PRAISE FOR PAT MULLAN

"Pat Mullan is a natural born storyteller with a gripping, engaging style. He may just be the next big thing in Irish crime fiction."

—Jason Starr, author of Lights Out.

"...has all the Irish gifts: dizzy narrative, sly humor, and marvelous readability."

—Ken Bruen,
Edgar and Macavity Award winning author of The Guards.

"Mullan is Ireland's answer to John Grisham, with a smattering of Ross MacDonald thrown in."

—JA Konrath, best-selling author.

"Mullan writes suspense with an edge reminiscent of Bob Ludlum. An author to watch."

—Cerri Ellis, Mostly Mystery Reviews.

"Pat Mullan is a mature and knowledgeable writer who puts together a thriller with the best of them. An author who can continue to capture his audience as long as he cares to try."

—Shelley Glodowski, MidwestBookReview.

"Pat Mullan's Last Days of The Tiger, is a razor blade down the spine. So fast-paced, expect whiplash. This is Irish noir with a hero whom you'll want at your back in any gunfight. Grab a copy and clear your schedule!"

—James Rollins,
New York Times bestselling author of Black Order.

"Good, tight writing, clean prose that just zips along, and characters that are engaging and memorable all contribute to a great book in the thriller genre."

—Peggy Vincent, Oakland, CA.

"You know you're reading a good thriller when you start to cast it for the movie before you've even finished."

—Eithne Hannigan, Bookreviews, Connemara Life magazine.

"The Circle of Sodom is an even mix of Crichton and Clancy and written equally as well. It's a classic page-turner and almost comes across as though it had been adapted from a screenplay."

—Review by Pod-dy Mouth.

A DEADLY GAMBLE

Pat Mullan

A Deadly Gamble

By Pat Mullan

ATHRY
HOUSE

An ATHRY HOUSE book

Copyright © 2015 Pat Mullan

ISBN-13: 978-0983865247
ISBN-10: 0983865248

Cover design by BEAUTeBOOK
Image Credits: stephane @ Flickr and Frank Kovalcheck @ Flickr

For Jean, *again...*

The Gambler

One

Miami

Elena Himmler-Ramos stood on her tiptoes and twirled a full circle, surrounded by floor to ceiling mirrors. Pleased and excited, she rushed across to the man seated in the black leather chair.

"Oh, Pierre, it's perfect," she gushed as she framed her hair with her hands.

"Ma chère Madame, it has to be perfect! It must be the best for you. After all, this is going to be the most magnificent day of your life."

Pierre was the best hairstylist in Miami, and in Paris. Few clients could expect, or afford, his services in their own home. Elena Himmler-Ramos was one of the few who could. The only daughter of the wealthiest family in Paraguay, she and her two brothers had been raised in Miami; dual citizenship, bought and paid for. Her family owned the H-R Group of companies, with interests in everything from oil to banking. Headstrong and rebellious, she had left a trail of broken engagements behind her. But now she had met her match.

She saw Pierre out and went back to her dressing room, stopping briefly to run her finger, sensuously, down the photo frame of Roger Coleman, her husband to be. Oh yes, the family would have preferred a match with money. They wanted the Greek shipping magnate. But that engagement, like so many others, died in their willful head-on clashes. No, Roger had no millions but he had style and grace and breeding. And she was in love, for the first time in her life. But she did not know that this was a union not to be. At that very moment her two brothers, Carlos and Eduardo, were striding, grim-faced, through the lobby of the Hilton Hotel on their way to Roger Coleman's room.

From a distance, Roger Coleman could easily be mistaken for George Clooney. His looks, his manufactured Oxford education and his Anglo-American accent immediately opened all the doors to the best places and the best people. It had been the same with the door into the H-R Group. And now his marriage to Elena would give him the wealth he never had and always wanted. Congratulating himself on his achievement, he walked to the bar and poured himself a scotch as the doorbell rang. Glass in hand, not expecting anyone, he opened the door, surprised to see Elena's brothers standing there.

"Carlos! Eduardo! Didn't expect to see you guys before the big day."

Unsmiling, they walked past him into the room. He closed the door, alarm bells ringing in his head.

"There isn't going to be any big day, Roger!" said Carlos.

Putting his glass down, Roger Coleman tensed, sensing danger in the room, yet still in disbelief.

"Carlos, what are you talking about? Is this some kind of a bad joke?"

Eduardo spoke this time, "Yes, it is one fucking bad joke! And you are the joker! You almost got away with it, didn't you Roger? But you screwed up. No Oxford education. No upper class family. You're a con man, a fraud. And you were about to pull off the biggest con job of your life, weren't you?"

Roger picked up his glass again, trying to look in control. Inside he knew the game was up. But he had to defend himself, deny everything, "What the hell are you talking about? That is absolute nonsense!"

Eduardo stood with his hands clenched into fists. Roger could see the anger on his face and the hatred in his eyes. Carlos had distanced himself from the confrontation. He stood at the window, looking out. Roger's protest hung in the air. And it died there. The scorn on Eduardo's face said enough. Finally he spoke again.

"We do not deal in nonsense. It was our duty to make sure we knew who Elena was bringing into our family. So we ran a thorough background check on you. Much of your background passed our security. Until we sent investigators to Oxford University. Yes, Roger Coleman attended Oxford and you have his academic record and his diploma. There's only one problem 'Roger'. The real Roger Coleman never left England. You thought nobody would find him because he's a paraplegic confined to a nursing home for the rest of his life. Everything about you is a fraud. But because of Elena we're letting you off easily. We want you out of the country now. Don't take anything. We have a car waiting to take you to the airport. You're booked on the next flight to London."

Roger Coleman realized that it was better to leave alive. So he opened the closet, took down his suitcase and packed the few clothes he had with him. He was traveling light.

Carlos and Eduardo escorted him out of the hotel to the waiting limo.

Two

Coleman was given no options at the airport. Armed with his passport, ticketed to London, and seat pre-selected, Carlos and Eduardo walked him to the boarding gate and waited until he had boarded the plane.

Once airborne, he ordered a double scotch, a small carton of milk and a glass. He poured the milk into the glass and added the scotch. Not a common drink. But it had always been his drink of choice. As he sipped, he seethed with anger. Anger at his own stupidity for choosing Coleman as his identity. Didn't believe anyone would find the real Coleman in his paraplegic state in that nursing home in Devon. He also didn't like to be pushed around and, long ago, he'd promised to never let that happen again. So he sat sipping his scotch and milk and contemplating his options. Calculating how to make Carlos and Eduardo pay. And pay they would. He considered his weapons. Knowledge. That was always the best weapon in any game. And he knew a lot about the Himmler-Ramos business and their banking relationships.

I guess they assumed that that would be of little value to me. That I'd walk away, lucky to still be standing. Well, they may have discovered that I am not who I said I was. But they failed to discover who I am. That will be their downfall.

The flight had one stopover in Atlanta and Coleman decided to get off there. He assumed that the Himmler-Ramos brothers would have someone at the Atlanta airport to prevent just that. But he also assumed that whoever it was, they'd never have met him personally and would be relying on photographs and descriptions to enable them to spot him. So he knew that he had to change what he looked like.

Three

Elena Himmler-Ramos walked out to the boat deck and looked across at the traffic on Arthur Godfrey Boulevard. A steady stream at eleven on this Saturday morning. All heading for Miami Beach.

She removed her sunglasses and held a soft white handkerchief against her red and angry eyes. Sore from a night's crying. Now the sadness had turned to anger. Anger at her brothers. Anger at the world. Anger at Roger. She loved him and she still loves him, she realizes. She doesn't really care if he's a pauper. But she's been threatened with disinheritance if she pursues him. And she knows that she would never survive if that happened.

She sat down on a deck chair and stayed there, almost trance-like, for the next hour. Then she got up, abruptly, and strode purposefully back to the house. In her bedroom, she walked into her clothes closet and pulled the wedding dress from its hanger. Armed with a pair of sharp scissors, she cut the dress into small strips. She didn't cry. She didn't feel anything. Finished, she bundled all the strips in her arms and walked out of her bedroom to the railings that overlooked the marble-floored entrance hallway. Then, with abandon, she opened her arms and let the pieces float like birds leaving a nest. Float and drift down to the ground below.

A catharsis, she thought.

Four

Sant Antoni, Ibiza

At the port of Sant Antoni Elena Himmler-Ramos stepped off the boat that had transported her from Barcelona. Karen and Denis Murphy waited for her. She ran to them, hugged Karen tightly and kissed Denis. They took her bags to their Range Rover and, within twenty minutes, they were at the door of their rose-hued home. On a hill overlooking the town, it was private and protected from the tourists and the night clubs. They took Elena's bags to her room and she followed. She'd been here before and knew that she would see the most stunning sunset from her large window.

Settled in, she joined Karen and Denis in their comfortable living room. Karen Brooks was the closest friend that Elena had. They had attended the University of Miami together and had become best friends. When Karen had fallen in love with Denis Murphy, Elena celebrated Karen's good fortune. Denis Murphy had made millions in telecoms and could afford the good life. Karen needed the good life. She couldn't imagine living without it.

She was here at their invitation. Here to purge Roger Coleman from her heart. The Murphys had brought her here for that purpose. They had met Coleman and had also been seduced by his charm. They had reveled in Elena's good fortune. Now they shared her disappointment. They hoped they'd be the therapy, the comfort, the recovery that she needed. But they had to have her open her soul here in Ibiza.

Cheese, fruit and wine 'broke the ice' and helped Elena to loosen her grip on her emotions. As tears welled up in her eyes, Karen held her hand and Denis refilled her glass. They felt that she had to talk about it without their prompts or encouragement. So they waited. Finally the flood-gates opened and she started to cry.

"I loved him. I think I still do."

Sally asked, "What happened?"

"I don't know. I don't know. Carlos and Eduardo said he was a fraud, a conman. They said that he'd stolen the name Roger Coleman. They sent him away. On my wedding day."

Karen held her until she could continue.

"He was kind, good to me. And he was smart and funny too. Always there for me. He was the best."

"We liked him too, Elena. We were sure you had found your soul-mate. So different from the others."

Elena let a forced smile slip through at that remark. She had indeed been unfortunate in love. Her previous two beaux had treated her badly. Cheated on her. They were only interested in what the Himmler-Ramos name could do for them. Carlos said that was all Roger was interested in too. But she never felt that with Roger. He was not the kind of man that Carlos said he was. That's why her heart was breaking.

"My heart is broken. I cut my wedding dress into ribbons and scattered it into the wind. To purge it all. But it didn't work."

"You have to forget him, Elena. You have to move on."

"I know. But I can't. I'd take him back now if he walked through that door."

"Well, we brought you here to help you to get over him. And we're going to force you to enjoy life while you're with us. We're only here for a week so let's make it count."

Elena dabbed her eyes with a handkerchief. She knew why she had come to Ibiza. But she also knew that she couldn't run away from herself. So she decided that she must let the Murphys in, let them try to help.

"Have you discussed this with your family?"

"No!"

"You've refused to face them?"

"I haven't spoken to my brothers since they broke up my wedding day. I hate them."

"But they didn't have a choice, did they?"

"There are good ways and bad ways of doing something. They chose the bad way."

Karen simply nodded her head, in agreement yet seeking an explanation. Elena continued:

"I did not know the wedding was off. I waited and waited and no-one showed up. Carlos and Eduardo were trying to punish me. They blamed me for almost bringing Roger into our family."

"And you didn't go home to Paraguay?"

"No. I felt that I was an outcast."

Karen and Denis had finally begun to realize the challenge they faced. They had had no inkling that Elena was in such a dire state. They decided that they had let Elena expose herself enough for the time being. They planned to do nothing but pamper her for the coming week. And that's exactly what they did.

At the end of the week, they announced, "Tomorrow evening we're going to watch the sunset from the Café Del Mar."

They arrived early enough to get a prized table on the best deck of the Café Del Mar. Sipping their cocktails and listening to very relaxing music, they watched the sun set into the crystal clear Balearic ocean. As the DJs cranked up the music and the decks got crowded, they soaked it all in. Elena felt herself transported to a parallel universe, one where no Roger Coleman ever existed. His purging had begun.

A Deadly Gamble

One

New York

Jim Sharkey woke up in an apartment in Lower Manhattan and didn't know how he got there. A body lay beside him. Dark and fat. Naked to the waist. Not a pretty sight. But must have looked good to him last night. Pictures flashed across his head like bursts from a damaged video. At the bar in Costelloe's. Taking a joint – he didn't even like the stuff – from the Englishman. Must have picked her up there. No, not there. She picked him up. Don't remember where. Just flashes of leathery skin and her yelling at him to squeeze her nipples. *Hard, hard, harder again*, she yelled. Yeah, crazy, he remembered that alright.

Looked at his watch. *Shit, it's noon time!* Looked at her. Out like a baby. Got dressed, didn't even shower, picked up his things and left. Once outside he saw the street sign and realized he was on 19th Street. He walked to the newsstand on the corner. He needed a paper. Maybe the deal had gone wrong. He flipped the pages. Nothing. Not a word. He relaxed, took a deep breath, and immediately froze. This was Wednesday's paper! A missing day! What the hell happened to Tuesday? He'd been in Costelloe's on Monday night. He'd lost an entire day. *Holy shit!*

He hailed a taxi, telling the driver to drop him at 60th and first. Only one place to go: Jack Miller's.

Crossing Park Avenue, he looked up at the forty stories of MetroBank, reminding himself that he'd once occupied a prized corner office on the 34th floor. Reminding himself that it had all started to go bad when Sally had walked out two years ago.

Jim Sharkey was a youthful forty-four. It belied the twenty years he'd spent at MetroBank. He joined MetroBank right after his army service, climbing from a trainee position to Vice President with a million dollar credit signature. He'd moved up through the ranks by attaching himself to rising stars who were part of a power network in the organization. As they climbed the ladder, he hitched a ride. But the power networks collapsed and the rising stars quit. Sharkey was left naked, with no political base for protection.

He'd also sacrificed his family. Long hours, unplanned overnight stays, missed birthdays, forgotten anniversaries, all made him unwelcome in his own home. His kids became strangers. His career started to collapse. Sally took the kids and left. They sold the house and he gave her everything. His lawyer advised against it but he wouldn't be dissuaded. So he ended up where he had started, twenty years earlier, in a studio apartment in Tribeca.

A year later, he lost his credit signature and his position. He was moved to a cubicle in the back office with no staff, not even a secretary. The organization chart showed him in a box called 'special projects'. Everyone knew that 'special projects' was a euphemism for the penalty box where executives went before they were forced to resign.

Jim never missed his Friday nights in Costelloe's. Tucked away at the corner of 50th Street and Second Avenue, Costelloe's entrance almost begged for anonymity. Carved out of an old brownstone building, the faded canvas awning covered a dimly lit entrance set well in from the street. The proprietor, Big Jim Connolly, always greeted him as he entered. Costelloe's acted like a private club and felt like home to Jim Sharkey. The regular members were a cross-section of Manhattan, from writers to actors to lawyers to bankers and business people, with the occasional *femme fatale* to add sexual tension to the ambience, already one of intrigue.

That's where Jack Miller had entered his life.

Jim usually drank alone and seldom got involved with any of the regulars. He knew them all, the famous and the unknown, and was happy to keep his relationship with them to his Friday nights. But it became different with Jack Miller. Miller was a new face at Costelloe's, said he'd only dropped in by accident when he'd moved uptown to the neighborhood. Tall, dark haired and square-jawed, a natural raconteur with an easy smile, quick to buy a round of drinks, he soon endeared himself to the regulars. On his first visit, a busy night at Costelloe's, he squeezed himself beside Jim at the bar and, before the night ended, he had learned all about Jim Sharkey while divulging little of himself, other than that he was a partner in a law firm.

Four weeks after they met, Jack Miller invited Jim to dinner one evening and he readily accepted. It beat a microwave meal in his apartment.

After the second gin and tonic, Jack cut to the chase, "Jim, I've got a sweet deal for you. How would you like to walk away from MetroBank with a couple of million?"

Stunned and feeling good from the g and t's, Jim said, "Quit bullshitting me. It's not funny. You know I've got maybe six months left. And I won't be getting any golden handshake."

"Easy! Easy! I'm not fucking around with you. I have a proposition to make. It's a selfish one. If we pull it off we'll both make millions. I'm not doing this for your benefit. I can't do it without you. And I've made a judgement call on this. I'm trusting you. I think you're ready for this deal."

By now Jim had willed himself to sober up. Miller's words bounced around his head, passing through experienced territory up there. He'd pushed back his glass and now sat upright in his chair.

"And if we don't pull it off?"

"Come on Jim, we can't fail. And I'll prove to you that nobody will be able to trace it to us. Anyway, we're only liberating ill-gotten gains. It's well known that money goes where it's treated well. And we can treat it well!."

"You're talking in riddles."

"OK. I'll spell it out for you. Here's the deal."

The deal was elegant. Miller said that his law firm represented a high net worth client in Paraguay and he had solid evidence that the client was the grandson of a prominent Nazi that even the great Simon Wiesenthal had been unable to track down. The family's fortune had been founded with Nazi funds, sourced from the rape and pillage of Europe. The Himmler-Ramos Group's Florida commercial bank used MetroBank as its correspondent bank. Miller proposed intercepting H-R funds transfers through MetroBank's computer system in New York and redirecting the funds to accounts that he had already set up in New York and Los Angeles, under false names, one for himself and one for Sharkey. He'd also opened two accounts in the Cayman islands. They'd transfer the money out of the country once they'd succeeded. Miller would get the New York account and Sharkey the LA account. That would put him close to Central America. He could move the money, take some in cash, and disappear across the Mexican border. No-one would be the wiser!

For a banker, Sharkey did not give Miller's plans the acid test. He had grown to believe Miller. That was his big mistake.

Miller was using the two account tactic to give credibility to Sharkey's equal share. But Miller had no intention of honoring that. He already had an account in the Cayman islands. One that he'd established years before. One that he used to move funds out of the States when it became too hot to move funds directly to his numbered Swiss account. After

2009 Swiss wire transfer regulations no longer made it possible for anonymous wire transfers to be received legally in Switzerland. Miller's Swiss account pre-dated these regulations so his Swiss account manager regarded Miller as being grandfathered in their privacy. So minimal effort was expended to meet the new regulations. Miller also had a long standing account in the Isle of Man. For tax avoidance purposes in the UK. Or tax evasion purposes. It would take an intricate trail to determine which.

Miller was persuasive, "It's blood money. The bastards don't deserve it."

"But I've never even stolen an apple off a fruit stand. I can't get my head around this."

"MetroBank screwed you! And now they're forcing you out after all your years of hard work, all your loyalty. For Christ's sake, they even cost you your family. I can't do this without you. I can provide the customer accounts and identification but only you can get your hands on their passwords and execute the funds transfers. Only you can do that."

"It's not as easy as you think."

"You told me they shoved you into a back office cubicle but you also told me that they haven't taken away your top level security clearance. That's their mistake. You can get to a funds transfer terminal. All you need is a supervisor's password, the customer's id and passwords, and your system's protocol and you're in."

"But they'll spot the transfer right away and the Feds will move in and freeze the accounts."

"No! Millions are transferred in and out of that Paraguay account every day. It'll be days, maybe weeks, before they catch on. Check it out. MetroBank has raised the limit on their transactions to the max, four million. You should only need to divert two transfers. That's eight million, four for me and four for you."

Jim didn't reply. He thought about it and decided that he'd examine the transaction history of that account when he went to the office next day. He needed to confirm what Miller was telling him.

"Even if I wanted to, I'm not sure if I could pull it off."

"OK, why not do a dry run? Check it out over the next few days. See if you can get the funds transfer system passwords that you'll need. Find a terminal you can use. Test that nothing is traceable to you. OK?"

Jim agreed. *What have I got to lose? Not a fucking thing,* he thought! And he already knew enough about MetroBank's funds transfer system to give him the sense that he could pull it off. Getting the supervisor's password would be dead simple for him. He'd do the dry run. *Nothing to lose,* he told himself, *not a fucking thing!*

Two hours later, they left the restaurant. Jim's heart was racing and it wasn't from the g and t's, the excellent wine, or the after dinner cognacs. It was from the audacity and sheer brilliance of the deal that Jack Miller had just spelled out. A deal, which, if executed right, would set him up for the rest of his life, and, if executed wrong, would also set him up for life, in a federal prison. He understood risk. He'd signed million dollar loan deals on behalf of MetroBank and he understood the risk each time. But he also knew that, if the deal went sour, the credit loss would be absorbed by MetroBank, not himself. If anything went wrong on this deal, he would absorb the risk. And it wouldn't be a financial penalty he'd suffer.

Two

Next day Jim Sharkey did indeed test the veracity of Jack Miller's information about his Paraguayan client. Millions flowed freely in and out of the account, transfers from and to every point in the globe. On certain days, the majority of financial transactions originated in the middle east, Abu Dhabi and Oman. He wondered about that and then dismissed it.

Who cares what these people are up to! Jack's right. This money needs a home, a place where it'll be well treated!

He decided there and then to do the deal.

That weekend he executed a *dry run*. He hadn't done a wire transfer in years, not since his days in operations. But the system hadn't changed in all that time. It was new then, state of the art, and it had stood the test of time.

He met Jack Miller for coffee early Monday morning to finalize everything.

"Brilliant! I knew you could pull it off."

"OK, I said you were right. It'll work and I don't see any way that they can trace it to me. I'll use supervisors' passwords and I'll do it next weekend when I can get to a terminal without anyone seeing me."

"So the money should be in our accounts by this time next week."

"About those accounts …"

"Don't worry. You'll have both account numbers. One's here in New York at Citibank and one's in LA at Bank of America. The identity is good, birth certificate, social security, credit card, and a passport. I'll have it ready for you. You'll be William Johnson, by the way."

They both agreed to give Costelloe's a miss on Friday and meet again after Jim had moved the money.

Three

Jack Miller looked at his bedside clock. Eight a.m. He lifted Inga's hand from his chest, climbed out of bed and crossed the room to his desk. He powered up his laptop, went on-line and entered the Citibank website. Entering his user name and password he waited as the screen displayed the account of Sam Smithberg, the name he'd used to open the New York account. It confirmed that two of the many transactions executed overnight had successfully transferred four million dollars into the account. He logged off and logged onto the account he'd set up at Bank of America in LA. This one under the name of William Johnson. Once again the screen confirmed two transfers in, two million each. Rubbing his hands with glee, he left Inga asleep, made himself a quick coffee, checked that he had the Sam Smithberg and William Johnson identifications, dressed and left.

At nine a.m. he entered the Park Avenue and 53rd Street branch of Citibank, presented his identity, and transferred four million dollars from Sam Smithberg's account to his Cayman Islands account. He walked a few blocks to Bank of America and transferred the four million from William Johnson's LA account to his Cayman Islands account. That done, he popped into the nearest travel agent and booked himself on the next flight to London. He also bought a ticket to Las Vegas for James Sharkey and made a reservation at Caesar's Palace.

By eleven a.m. he was back in his apartment, watching Inga step, dripping wet, out of the shower. He tore his clothes off, pushed her back inside, turned on the shower and closed his eyes as she directed the fine spray over his head, his chest, finally settling lower as he rose in anticipation.

Later he sat at his desk, pulled a manila envelope out of a drawer, put fifty-thousand dollars, the confirmed reservation at Caesar's, and the airline ticket to Vegas into it. Finally he wrote a note to Jim and dropped it in. The broad was well paid to ensure Sharkey got enough to keep him out of commission for a couple of days. *Strictly a loser*, mused Miller, without a single feeling of remorse.

He gave the envelope to Inga, telling her to give it to Jim when he showed up and telling her to tell him that he'd meet him in Las Vegas.

A few hours later he sat in first class, watching Long Island disappear below.

Four

The taxi dropped Jim Sharkey at 60th and First. He shoved some bills into the driver's hand and didn't wait for the change. Minutes later he stepped off the fourth floor elevator, walked to Miller's apartment and rang the doorbell.

A healthy looking twenty-something blonde opened the door. Said, in a sultry foreign accent, "Jack is not here."

"Where is he?"

Sharkey didn't wait for an answer, just went past her into the living room.

"What's your name?"

"Inga."

He wasn't really interested. He didn't want to swap bios, war stories, or bodily fluids with her.

But she persisted.

"I had nowhere to stay. Jack let me stay here. As long as I need, he said. Jack is very kind. Are you a friend of Jack? Are you Jim?"

"Yeah, I'm Jim."

"Jack left something for you. He said to make sure I gave it to you when you showed up."

She walked over to the bookcase, reached between the books, retrieved a large manila envelope and gave it to him.

"Can I get you a drink?"

Seeing the Chivas whisky and glasses on the bureau, he answered.

"Good idea. Chivas. On the rocks."

One in the afternoon was earlier than usual for him. But what the hell. This was not a usual day. As she fixed his drink, he opened the envelope and a package of money slid into his lap. He slit the binder and counted fifty-thousand dollars. He reached inside and found an airline ticket to Las Vegas and a reservation at Caesar's Palace. And a note from Jack:

> *Jesus, Jim, couldn't find you anywhere. Did you shack up with that broad? Deal executed perfectly! Small change of plan. Figured we must celebrate. Meet me in Vegas. Then you can pick up your stuff in LA and live happily ever after!*
>
> *Jack.*

No paperwork for William Johnson and no info for LA account. He'd expected Jack to have that ready to go, as promised. He picked up the phone and called Jack's cell. No answer. He tried again. No answer, just Jack's voice inviting the caller to leave a message. Jim didn't bother.

Guess he's saving it for Vegas, he reckoned. The flight was due to leave at five o'clock, in four hours' time. He downed the Chivas, abandoned Inga, and caught another taxi on First Avenue, telling the driver to take him to Tribeca. When he got there, he asked the taxi driver to wait for him, bounded into his apartment and packed a case with his best jacket and pants, his cool Jack Murphy shoes, said goodbye to the place, and minutes later sat in the taxi on his way to the airport.

Five

London

Roger Coleman hailed a cab at Heathrow and exited onto the M4 for London. It's been six years, he thought, but it feels like slipping into an old glove. Must be at home. The cockney cab driver rambled on about the weather, the traffic, the dirty deeds of London's politicians, the latest football results, the financial rip-offs. Soon discovering that his passenger never answered his questions, at first Coleman became irritated but, incapable of turning the cabdriver off, he settled for the ramble as background noise, part of the price paid for ending up with a loquacious Cockney driver. He sat deep into his seat and let the traffic on the M4 lull him into a trance, one that brought his life flashing like a video in front of his eyes. He'd left Jack Miller behind him in New York. A necessary identity. One that has enriched him more than any con game had ever done. For a moment he wished that he'd be there when Carlos and Eduardo discovered their missing millions. And, of course, he was sure they'd never connect him to it. Only that schmuck Sharkey. What a loser. But they'd hit a dead end there too. He paid old Bruce in Vegas very well to take care of it all. And he knew Bruce would do anything if well compensated. Only one thing made him feel remorse.

Selfish remorse. The loss of Elena. She genuinely loved him. He believed that. Who knows, maybe we'll cross paths again, he dreamed.

Time to leave Roger Coleman behind him too. Still, the name had served him well. Got him into the States. And enabled Himmler-Ramos to covert his forty-five day visa into a work permit and eventually into a resident green card. With his criminal convictions and time in prison, he'd never have gotten a visa in his own name. But the Coleman name had to go. The Himmler-Ramos brothers had discovered the identity theft.

Within the hour, he'd reached Knightsbridge and turned into Sloane Street. He directed the driver to pull up outside the Cadogan Hotel. He had a reservation for the next seven days. In his own name: Tom Gordon-Smith. He owned an apartment in London but he had not seen it since he left. He needed to settle matters with Big Ned Simms and make peace with his father before he moved back in again.

He dropped his bag in the corner of his room and took out his laptop. Connected to the hotel's wifi, he brought up his Cayman Island bank, entered his password, and made two money transfers: four million dollars to his numbered Swiss account and four million to his account in the Isle of Man. Next he phoned Sam Bell, his personal account manager at his bank in Douglas in the Isle of Man, giving him a 'heads up' on the funds transfer. He also told Sam that he'd be there in two days to withdraw three million. At the exchange rate that would amount to almost two million sterling. A healthy sum.

His watch said seven-thirty a.m. But he was still on US time; to him, it was only two-thirty a.m. He hadn't slept on the flight. Jetlagged and dead tired, he climbed out of his clothes and sank under the sheets.

Six

Las Vegas

One-arm bandits stood at attention at McCarron airport. Official greeters, Las Vegas style. But Sharkey'd been here before, so no surprise.

The cabby boasted that he was a blackjack dealer by night and a cabby by day. Another story of the illusory dream. He dropped him at Caesars and Jim tipped him well.

They were expecting him this time. His reservation was ready and the computer screen, at the registration desk, flashed 'VIP'. In other words: *big gambler, treat well.*

Jack had sure loaded the dice for him. It was obvious. The clerk's look of indifference suddenly changed to a huge smile of welcome. A young man rushed to get his bags and take him to his room.

His room! Take that back! More like a suite in Caesar's ancient Rome. It was in the Fantasy Tower. Circular Jacuzzi bathtub in the center of the bedroom. Huge circular bed, surrounded by a floor to ceiling diaphanous screen. A large circular mirror on the ceiling reflected the bed.

Sharkey thought that it didn't get any better than this. He was wrong. It did. Better came by the name of Maria. Exotic. Spanish blood, maybe.

"They told me to take care of you," she said, as she started to run a bath for him, "You must be tired from your journey. A bath and a massage is just what you need."

She stayed to watch him undress.

The Jacuzzi bubbled gently as he eased himself in, sat back, stretched his toes out to feel the jets, and looked up at Maria. She was undressing. Slowly. Just for his benefit.

Maria stepped into the Jacuzzi and eased her body between his legs. In moments a young female attendant appeared with a bottle of Montrachet in a silver ice bucket. She poured two glasses, and then left the room.

Soon he felt very tired, unable to keep his eyes open. He could see Maria through a haze but he had a sense that the lights were going out and the room was turning dark, dark as midnight. Panic forced its way into his remaining consciousness and his heart began to race. He tried to get up but his legs wouldn't cooperate. He imagined that he could see Maria, standing back with a smile on her face. Somehow, with a superhuman effort, he managed to heave himself over the edge of the Jacuzzi.

As he hit the floor all the lights went out, and before he slid into darkness, his brain screamed one word in agony: *screwed!*

Seven

London

Startled, Tommy Gordon-Smith woke up. His phone was ringing. Disoriented, it took time to realize where he was.

Reaching across, he grabbed the phone and answered, groggily, "Yeah?"

"Hey, Tommy, it's me, Bruce."

In that fog between sleep and wakefulness, for a moment he did not know who Bruce was. But, just as suddenly, the fog disappeared.

"Sorry, Bruce, still asleep. A day later and I'm still jetlagged. It's a bitch!"

"I expected that. But I thought you'd need to know. The 'package' arrived safely. And it's been re-cycled, as agreed."

Tommy let the news sink in. With Sharkey out of the way, he was free and clear. Nothing should lead the Himmler-Ramos people to him.

"Good. Glad we're taking care of the environment."

They chatted, usual small talk, for a minute or two. Then Bruce hung up. His mission accomplished, the contract filled, his friend protected, there was no more to say.

Tommy stood, lost in thought. The past suddenly seemed like yesterday.

Those were the days my friend
We thought they'd never end
We'd sing and dance forever and a day
We'd live the life we choose
We'd fight and never lose
For we were young and sure to have our way.

The lyrics came from nowhere. And he was transported back sixteen years. Vegas 1998. Carefree and bulletproof, he could feel the wind rushing through his hair as he put his foot to the pedal and felt his red convertible whiz through Vegas, the casino signage melding into a Jackson Pollock canvas. Adrenalin pumping and anticipation surging, he was heading for one of Bruce's hot parties. His dad had made the final table at the World Series of Poker. Yeah, *Golden Tom,* that's what they called his old man. Holder of two bracelets, he'd become a regular at the Vegas poker tables. And every time he came, every year now for the past four, he'd bring Tommy Jr. with him.

Ever since I was twenty, thought Tommy. *And I've been part of Bruce's good life in Vegas ever since I was twenty.*

Two valets rushed forward as he swung his car round the circular driveway and came to a full stop. Bruce always provided valet parking when he held one of his big parties. The shorter, more assertive, of the two, won. Smartly holding the driver's door open, he held out his hand for the keys. With a big '*thank you, sir*' and a wide toothy grin, he slid behind the steering wheel. Tommy watched him with some trepidation as he accelerated rapidly and drove away to the parking lot.

Crossing the thresh-hold, peals of laughter and screams of excitement greeted him from the party already well underway by the pool.

You're overdressed, darling! The words flowed silkily from Cheryl's pouting lips. Barefooted, she walked toward him. Topless. Light red hair, a face that could seduce any man, and a body that simply said: *we've broken the mold on this one. Not entirely true*, he corrected himself, *they used the same mold on her twin sister, Cherise.*

He said, *you're certainly not overdressed, Cheryl,* as she snuggled her body against him. *Wait. You are Cheryl, aren't you?* She pulled back in laughter. Pointing to her right breast, she said, *Cherise doesn't have a mole like this.* She pulled away, ran toward the pool, jumped in and enticed him to follow.

The pool area was crowded with beautiful people in various stages of undress. A young man circled with a tray of drinks and held it out to him. He picked one off the tray, left it at poolside and started to undress.

He could see Bruce waving to him. Prostrate on a lounger, attended by three beautiful young ladies, he was the image of a young Hugh Hefner. *This is Playboy Mansion, Vegas Style,* thought Tommy. He jumped in and joined Cheryl in the already crowded pool.

Later, much later, after a day and evening that ended in a bed somewhere in the bowels of Bruce Morgan's sprawling villa, Cheryl appeared in the adjoining bathroom door, silhouetted against the steamy shower light. For a moment he saw two images of her but then he knew it was the booze making him see double. But when Cheryl crawled into bed facing him and Cherise arched her body against his back, he knew he'd gone to heaven.

Something brought him back to the present. The lyrics echoed somewhere in his head. *Those were the days my friend. We thought they'd never end.* He looked at the time. It was two p.m. Feeling good about himself, he headed for the shower, thinking: *clean up, hit the town, celebrate, life is good.*

Eight

Mousey Sinclair gulped down her second gin and tonic, an appetizer for the rest of the evening. She liked to drop in to *The Bunch of Grapes* in Knightsbridge from time to time. Especially when she was nostalgic for the past. But this was no longer her local and she had to ride the underground from her flat in Fulham to get here. And she hated the underground. Squeezed into a corner of this very busy pub, she felt cosseted by the throng, strangely reminiscent of the fans who used to throng around her at every appearance.

Gemma Sinclair had once been the most beautiful girl in London. She had everything: good looks, good breeding, aristocratic English grandmother, self-made Scottish grandfather, best public school education. But she had one incurable weakness. She was in love with Tommy Gordon-Smith. Despite his ego, his gambling, his questionable enterprises, his frequent embarrassing appearances on the front pages of the tabloids. Yes, despite all that, Gemma Sinclair was inextricably in love with Tommy Gordon-Smith. She began to share the sleazy pages of the tabloids with him. Her family disowned her. She didn't care.

So she was devastated when he told her that he had to flee. Had to leave the country. Said it was either that or fishing his body out of the Thames. One of his deals had gone terribly wrong. Cost his partners thousands. And his partners were the

East London Simms, a tribe regarded as the major criminal gang in the city. She couldn't verify the story. And she thought that, if he'd done that to the Simms, he'd never leave the country; his body would already be in the Thames. Said he'd send for her. Six months, he said. But six months came and went. And another six months came and went. And yet another. Gemma sought solace in the pain-killers of the day: cannabis, cocaine, heroin. In three years she'd lost her looks, her place in society, her friends. She slipped down the social ladder until she hit the bottom. She was no longer Gemma Sinclair. She became Mousey Sinclair. Her once beautiful face was gone. Her gums were red and her front teeth seemed about to fall out. In denial, she still managed to firm up her cheeks, retrieve the classic pout in her lips that once graced the covers of the best magazines.

She knew what the night would bring. Oblivion. Strangely comforting. Phil Collins' voice was struggling to be heard over the noise of the throng. Looking up, she saw young Paddy, the bartender who always looked out for her. He was pushing his way towards her, a carafe of house red in his right hand and a plate of hot food in his left.

"Got to get somethin' in yah, dear", coaxed Paddy.

"Oh, Paddy, I love you. You know that, don't you?" she slurred.

He bent over, kissed her on the cheek, and retreated back through the throng. Suddenly Mousey stood up. *It can't be,* she thought. Standing in the middle of a group of admirers, talking and laughing expansively. *Tommy Gordon-Smith.*

Her heart beat rapidly. She couldn't breathe. The lights started to flicker and go out. The room began to spin. She felt claustrophobic. Her heart started to flutter and skip beats. The room got darker. She lost consciousness and fell, striking her temple against the table as she went. Blood began to trickle down her cheek.

Tommy Gordon-Smith couldn't avoid the fuss in the pub when the ambulance crew arrived and placed the woman who had collapsed on a litter. As they squeezed their way out, he caught a glimpse of her. An eerie, oddly familiar memory awoke. *Gemma! Couldn't be. Not the lady I remember. Still, eerie though!* Guilt was an emotion that he had exorcised from himself. Besides, he thought, Gemma's probably living in luxury somewhere with a rich, devoted husband and three or four young kids. Leading the life she wanted. He shrugged it off and re-joined the banter at the bar. He missed the happening outside when the ambulance crew reached the street. Lights flashed in their eyes. A paparazzi. Got his photos and fled. Momentarily distracted, the ambulance crew moved her toward the waiting ambulance.

The ambulance crew made a judgment call a few minutes after Mousey Sinclair was lifted aboard. Unconscious, they called ahead and the trauma team waited their arrival at St. Mary's Hospital's major trauma center. One of the top trauma centers in London, they felt that she would get the best care there.

A consultant and the trauma team took charge of Mousey immediately. She had regained consciousness upon arrival. They checked her vital signs, ensured that her airway was clear, checked her neck veins for distension or collapse, and evaluated the external hemorrhage of her head. They inserted an IV, took blood, stabilized her head and neck and immediately took her to radiology for a CT scan to determine if there was any intracranial bleeding.

After all the examination and diagnosis was complete, they determined that she was suffering from concussion. Nothing more serious. But they decided that she needed close monitoring for at least forty-eight to seventy-two hours. They moved her to a bed in the trauma ward.

Nine

Isle of Man

As the British Airways City Flyer lifted off at noon from London City Airport, Tommy Gordon-Smith relaxed. He struggled to keep his eyes open. Something about his lingering jet-lag, his over indulgence in the pub, the physically and emotionally stressful recent weeks was catching up with him. *Just getting old*, he laughed to himself.

An hour and a quarter later, he braced himself for touch-down as the Saab 2000 turbo prop eased on to the runway at Ronaldsway Airport in the Isle of Man. Sam Bell sat in a limo waiting his arrival. Dependable and discreet, Sam knew that Tommy had always been very generous with him. He expected an extra generous tip on this transaction. Tommy saw him as soon as he left the main entrance to the airport. The driver held the door open for him.

"You don't look a day older", said Sam.

"Please, please … I sure do feel older."

And thinking that Sam had aged, balder and with middle-aged spread, he said, "Sam, what's your secret. You're still the same after five years!"

"Lying will get you everything" laughed Sam, "anyway, it's good to see you. We'll go to my office first. I have your withdrawal ready. We can complete the transaction there. Then I've booked lunch for us. Special sea food place. It's what we do best here in Mann."

Douglas had more banks than any other business. Complete privacy suited Tommy well. And he reckoned that Sam would have to be tortured before he revealed anything. Sam's bank operated in the shadows, in that it bore no well-known international, or national, banking name. That made it even more attractive to a client like Tommy. And Sam managed plenty of clients like Tommy Gordon-Smith.

"No banks hit the dust here."

"We don't play with risky financial deals. No securitized mortgage packages that were filled with sub-prime shit. And no market making deals that screw one client and reward another. No fancy credit swaps and contracts for difference."

"So you lead a boring life," laughed Tommy.

"Maybe I don't run around the world like you but I still get a thrill out of the day. You've brought that to me today. I'm curious as hell about what you've been up to. Lucrative, I'd say, given your healthy cash flow."

"You know I can't tell you, Sam. As the saying goes, *if I tell you I'll have to kill you.*"

Sam doubled over and howled with deep laughs. In a usually taciturn man, the image was a complete mismatch. Finally he composed himself, sat up straight and wondered if his driver had seen him in the mirror. So unbecoming, he thought. The car eased into his private parking slot. Saved by the driver, he thought.

Twenty minutes later, transaction completed, Sam gratefully acknowledged a most generous tip. Tommy picked up the attaché case that held his money, neatly prepared in small packets.

As promised Sam had arranged a lunch at his favorite seafood restaurant. Lunchtime ended at 2 but they had stayed open for Sam. Private and confidential. Tommy chose the very succulent scallops, the queenies, that Mann was prized for. He ordered and was not disappointed. The taste and texture lingered on his palate for the rest of the day.

He did not fly back to London. He took the ferry to Heysham from the Sea Terminal in Douglas. At Heysham the limo he'd ordered was waiting. He sank into the plush seating, took a deep breath and closed his eyes. Then he became aware that he was still gripping the case with a closed fist. *Goddamit*, he screamed silently, *ease the fuck up!*

It was dark when he arrived back in London. He did not go directly to his apartment. Instead we went to his lock-up. A few blocks from his apartment, he had leased it for the past five years. It housed his E-Type jag, his favorite possession. Only one person knew about the lock-up and he was paid well to keep his mouth shut. Benny Willis, a fine mechanic, who kept the jag in good condition. He unlocked the door, slid it open, and closed it behind him. He switched on the light and patted the jag lovingly as he passed. At the end wall he moved a metal rack that sat on a well-worn square of old carpet. He picked up the carpet and exposed an iron wall safe embedded in the concrete floor. He turned the combination lock until it clicked and the door opened. He left half-a-million in the case and removed packets totaling the remaining million and a half, which he placed in the safe. He locked the safe, replaced the old carpet, and moved the metal rack back on top of it.

On the way out, he patted his jag again. *My touchstone*, he thought.

Ten

Wapping, London

"I should have you fucking killed, boyo!"

Big Ned Simms's body shook with anger. His eyes bulged and a dribble ran from the edge of his mouth. Tommy Gordon-Smith stood between the two Simms nephews. He was in Big Ned's house in Wapping. The nephews had escorted him in from the locked and barred wrought iron gate that bordered the street in front. Big Ned had watched him through his security monitor. Tommy had known that he had to settle with Big Ned. He could never live here again if he didn't.

"You're right! And I'd have felt that way too. But that deal collapsed. I didn't cheat you. I lost big ..."

"You ran out on me. You left the sinking ship, boyo!"

"I had to."

"Yeah, bullshit, where were you hidin'?"

"Miami, Paraguay, New York."

Big Ned had to admit a degree of astonishment to himself. But he dare not show that. So he shuffled back and forth for a minute.

"So, where is it?"

Tommy picked up his leather carry bag and handed it to Big Ned who walked around the table, placed it down and opened it. His expression changed instantly from one of anger to one of, if not pleasure, contentment.

"There's half a million in there. That's twice what you lost."

Big Ned said nothing. Instead he took out a packet of sterling and thumbed it till he had the count. Then he counted the number of packs in the bag. Half a million. Confirmed. He walked over to Tommy.

"Good! But not enough. That quarter of a mill that you cheated me out of could have been working for me. And it would have been a hell of a lot more today."

"You don't know that. Half a mill is good money."

"I told you. One million or nothing, boyo!"

Tommy knew this would happen. He had to try and get away with the half mill. But he was prepared to give Big Ned what he wanted.

Big Ned smiled. He reached out and put his big arm across Tommy's shoulder, "Listen, boyo. This is a good faith down payment. You bring me the other half mill and I'll welcome you back again."

He laughed loudly, "You'll be a fully paid up member again! And all your privileges will be restored."

He was still laughing loudly as the nephews escorted Tommy out.

As soon as the nephews returned, he looked at them and said,

"Once bitten, twice shy. I don't trust this boyo. So I want you to stick to him like glue. If it looks like he's reneging on this deal, I need to know. Immediately. Don't fail me!"

Eleven

London, St. Mary's Hospital

Two days in the trauma ward was too much for Mousey Sinclair. She got angry with the nurses, talked in her sleep, irritated the nearest patients.

She wanted a drink. Badly.

She hurt deep inside. Depressed, sad and angry, she wanted revenge. She wanted to hurt Tommy Gordon-Smith, wanted to see him pay for what he had done to her.

Fists clenched, head buried under her pillow, she did not hear the voice. Not until a hand removed the pillow.

"Ms. Sinclair. I am Doctor Shepard."

Mousey struggled into a sitting position, bolstered by pillows. She nodded an acknowledgment.

"I am going to discharge you today."

Mousey smiled and uttered a silent 'thank you'.

"But you need to know that you are in danger. Next time you have an accident like this, you may not get off so lightly."

Mousey said nothing. Tried her best to look solemn.

"You have inflammation of the liver. Mild hepatitis at this point. You are drinking too much. This is a warning. If you don't change your habits, you will damage your liver."

Mousey finally acknowledged, "Yes, I know Doctor."

"You need help. But only you can ask for it. I can't force you to seek help. I'll leave this card with you. When you're ready, call them. They'll help you to take that first step."

Mousey took the card and thanked the doctor. An hour later she stood at the door of the hospital, examining a tube map. She needed to get to Barons Court station, the closest stop to her Hammersmith flat. Gone were the days when she was flush with money and could easily afford a cab.

Twelve

The Daily Scoop

Sandy Thomas walked onto the floor of his newspaper. A hub of activity clustered around three desks in the center. Noisy conversation dominated. The editor, Frankie Scott, looked animated. Young, brilliant, articulate, ambitious, he strode around the desks, tie loosened, sleeves rolled up, shirttail hanging out, dirty blond hair ruffled. They were arguing over the cover and the editorial. Frankie spotted Sandy and shouted, "See you in my office in twenty."

Sandy walked to the coffee machine in the corner, poured a strong cup and crossed to his desk. He removed the camera from his bag, connected it to his computer, clicked and offloaded his latest collection. He selected the two most recent, those that he had taken of Gemma Sinclair on the litter outside *The Bunch of Grapes* in Knightsbridge. He cropped and enhanced them. Then he reflected on the pitch he would make to Frankie Scott. It was a dangerous time for the media. There was a witch hunt on, especially against popular media like *The Daily Scoop*, derogatively referred to as tabloid journalism. Tabloid sized newspapers like the *National Enquirer*, *Globe*, *The Sun*, *The Daily Scoop* were the prey.

The *News of the World* had already fallen victim and Rupert Murdoch had closed it following extensive investigations about phone tapping. But Sandy saw an opportunity and he was anxious to sell it to Scott.

Half an hour later Sandy sat waiting in Frankie Scott's office as he stormed in, a ham sandwich half in his hand and half in his mouth,

"My lunch. You've got fifteen minutes Sandy to get my attention."

"I won't waste your time. But I can see you in a hot debate over your cover story, your editorial, the paper's direction. Am I right?"

"Alright, smart-alec. I have to appear before this government investigating committee about phone tapping at nine am tomorrow. I know we didn't tap any phones but they don't believe that. I don't want to change the *Scoop's* direction but, right now, I need to cover my arse."

"But we can look at all this as an opportunity. *The News of The World* is gone, leaving a huge gap in the market. We can fill that gap!"

"Ok. You've got ten minutes left," said Frank as he scoffed down the remainder of his sandwich.

Sandy opened his laptop and turned the screen to face Frankie. He clicked on the last shot, a close-up of Gemma on the litter. Frankie looked at it without immediate comment. Sandy knew he had his attention. A silent response was always a sign of Frankie's attention.

"Who is she?"

"Gemma Sinclair."

Frankie looked again and remained unconvinced. Gemma Sinclair's face had been burned into the brain of every media-hip professional in London. Five years ago, she was the number one prey of the paparazzi. Stunningly beautiful, she graced the covers of all the major magazines. Then she disappeared.

"Can't be."

That's all Frankie said. He really wanted Sandy to confess that it wasn't her. He did not want to see her in this state.

"Trust me. It's her. She's lost it all. Almost in the gutter, she is!"

"That's unbelievable."

"And that's my pitch. I want to create a new human interest segment for *The Daily Scoop*. Not daily, probably weekly, in instalments. I'd like to call it: *Where Are They Now?* It's not original. It's been done before. ITV television series, for example. And always successful. But I want to give it a new twist. One that suits us. We'd only follow people who have fallen all the way to the bottom. And we'd deliver their story in weekly instalments, to capture and retain the readership."

Sandy could see the wheels turning in Frankie Scott's nimble brain and he knew he had him hooked. So he immediately followed up to close the deal.

"Gemma Sinclair will be our first story. I know she's not Hollywood but she was the top local personality, someone that everyone followed. I believe they will want to find out *where she is now*. And they will cry. People love stories of failure. And they'll buy our paper. I'll bet our circulation surges. And we won't have to tap anyone's phone for our stories."

Frankie looked at Sandy and smiled,

"I like it. I want to see the draft of Gemma's story, the segment mock-up, the brand image that we'll carry as a banner on the headings of our cover page. I want to see the whole shebang before I approve. And I want that one week from today."

Sandy thanked him, trying to hide his exuberance. He thought the one week deadline was too tight but it wouldn't be smart to contest that now. He knew he could deliver much of what Frankie wanted but he needed more time to produce the hot first segment of the Gemma Sinclair story.

Thirteen

Jim Sharkey woke to a blinding headache. He didn't know where he was, didn't remember a thing. He tried to ohis eyes but his eyelashes were stuck and his eyelids were sealed tight. He felt hard ground under him, tried to turn on his side and his arm hit something very hard, sending a sharp pain shooting up into his shoulder. The pain brought him fully awake. His throat felt parched and he traced his fingers over his cracked painful lips. *At least I'm not buck naked*, he thought as he felt the shirt and pants that he wore. Tucking his legs under him, he leveraged himself to a sitting position.

With the little saliva he could muster he wet his right sleeve and rubbed his eyes until he freed the hard mucous that held them closed. Forcing them open, he shaded them against the bright sunlight and looked around. He could see that he was on desert ground and he could feel the sun beat a hole in his head. Shading his eyes, he looked around. His jacket lay on top of a bunch of shrubs just a few feet away. He dragged himself there and picked it up. He patted his pockets and was surprised to find a bulge on the inside pocket of his jacket. A passport in the name of William Johnson and his wallet! He took it out, opened it, and gave it a cursory examination. Seemed OK, couple a hundred dollars, a few business cards, scribbled notes on pieces of paper. And his credit cards. He looked again and saw that he had two credit cards in his own name and one in William Johnson's name, the one that he'd gotten from Jack Miller. Guess they figured that it was best to lose all this with him.

Seeing that they don't expect me to survive. But they sure as hell didn't leave me the envelope with the rest of Jack's fifty grand! No, that would be really stupid! Not now! Not Now! Stay focused! Survive! Where's my cell phone, he suddenly thought. Hoping against hope, he frantically searched the jacket and the pants he was wearing. *Maybe it dropped out of my pocket.*

He searched, hands and knees all around the immediate area. Nothing. Exhausted, he gave up and sat down. He put the jacket over his head to ward off the sun and let his mind take over…and his mind took him back to his very last memory – slipping over the edge of the Jacuzzi in Caesars just as everything went dark. Now he felt angry, and stupid too. They had drugged him and dumped him out here in the desert. Probably last night after he fell out of the Jacuzzi. His jacket smelled of creosote. From the bush. Must be a creosote bush.

Means that I'm probably in the Mojave Desert because it's covered in creosote bush. That would put me south, maybe south-west of Vegas.

Dying of thirst, he looked around, hoping for water. Maybe a cactus he could cut open. But no cactus. And he chided himself because he had nothing to cut it open with even if he did come across one. *Why didn't they kill me?* No need to add murder. Just dump me out here in the middle of nowhere and they figured that I'd die of thirst, or dehydration, or snakebite, or whatever. The odds were against him getting out of here alive. But that thought only angered him. And took him back to his days in the Special Forces.

Shit, he thought, *I've been in tougher scrapes than this. But that was twenty years ago and now I'm soft and scared and worthless.*

But he didn't really believe that. Deep inside, he knew he had a strong backbone. Bravery. Not flaunted, not worn on his sleeve. Hidden, called into reserve when needed. For a moment his mind flashed back to the days when he needed it. When he used it. The Gulf, 1991. *Desert Storm. Desert Shield.* He remembered.

We thought it should have been called Desert Sucks. I was in the Marines that led the advance toward Kuwait City. We had moved at 4 am. From the border, a 20-kilometer march took us within five kilometers south of the minefield we were to breach when the ground offensive began. We blasted through the minefield and moved on, and struggled through deep, desert sand with heavy combat loads. In that first day of the war we advanced halfway to Kuwait City. But not without a fight. We were told that the Iraqis had been pulverized by air strikes and that we would encounter little resistance. But someone failed to tell that to an Iraqi mechanized division that had decided to stand and fight. Visibility was low in the desert but we could hear the unmistakable sound of track vehicles headed our way. We had nowhere to hide and there was no time to dig trenches. And we didn't know how many track vehicles we might be facing. Or what kind of track vehicles. Faced with no choice but to confront them head-on, we knew that we could be sitting ducks for the Iraqis. I remember it well. I lost all sense of fear, grabbed an AT4, a light anti-tank weapon, and moved blindly through the dust storm until I saw the tank. I knelt, fired, and watched it explode in front of me. The artillery fire we'd called in took out the trapped tanks and vehicles behind that first tank. We moved on. Past burnt out vehicles and dead bodies littering the ground.

Shit, that was a real desert! This is only a Hollywood back-lot of a desert, he yelled at the top of his voice. *Something primordial*, he thought, *about yelling to no-one in the middle of nowhere.* And recuperative. As a therapy, it worked!

He picked himself up and looked around. At least they'd left him his shoes. Even though what he really needed was a pair of those army desert boots he wore in the Gulf. *OK, let's do this by the numbers.* First, an inventory. He looked all around again. He only had the clothes he was wearing, the jacket and pants and shirt he was wearing when he had booked into Caesar's.

OK, where am I? He could see the clones of creosote bushes and short shrubs that dominated the area. Digging into his school geography lessons about the Nevada desert, one word came to mind. *Mojave. Yeah, my bet's on the Mojave Desert.*

What time is it? Shielding his eyes, he looked up. The sun had risen over the horizon and the desert had started to heat up. *Must be nine, ten, in the morning. They must have dumped me here in the middle of the night. By noon, this place will be sweltering, an oven! That's two, three hours away. And I have no water. There's supposed to be springs, oases, somewhere in the Mojave. I think. But maybe my mind is just inventing that to comfort me. Maybe I'll find a way to cut into a cactus.*

I must start walking out of here. In what direction? Well, it's either trying to find my way back to Vegas. Or heading for L.A. It's almost the toss of a coin. But no! It isn't! Going back to Vegas now is not a good idea! I need to find out what happened. I need to find out if Jack Miller screwed me. And it's best if they think I didn't survive. And I intend to survive!

He could feel the old warrior being re-born in himself. If his bet was right, he needed to be heading South West to reach the California state border. The sun had just risen in the east so he guessed if he headed due west and a little to the south of that, he should be positioned in the right direction.

Maybe I'll get lucky – run into an old prospector or someone. Ah well, it's fantasies like that that keep us going in life. Shit! No time to get philosophical! He covered his head with his jacket to keep the sun off and tied the arms together across his neck to hold it in place. Watching where he walked, he set out at a steady pace, heading south west.

Fourteen

Mojave Desert

Jim Sharkey stumbled, barely putting one foot after the other. He knew that, to stay alive, he had to keep going. The sun shone directly overhead. He was dehydrated and his mind played tricks with him. He was delirious. But he was determined to fight it.

Up ahead a ball of dust moved across the land. Maybe a mile away, he reckons. Then immediately dismisses the thought.

Could be half a mile, could be ten miles. Maybe it's a road, maybe it's a vehicle of some kind. Ah hell, it's probably a mirage, just like the ones I've seen all day.

He stumbled on, hoping against hope. He's no longer sure what direction he's headed. Could have been travelling in circles for the last hour for all he knows.

The road, the road, I need to get to the road.

But the delirium gets worse and he finds himself in the Gulf. At times he's not sure where he is.

Maybe it's one of their tanks! And where are all the guys in my platoon? Dead? Yeah, they're all dead!

He looks ahead through the miasma of his mind, sees the dust-ball getting closer. Now he's convinced it's the enemy.

He starts to run, looking for cover, trips, stumbles, throws his arms out to save himself. But his body wants to hit the ground and he knows he can't stop it. In seconds his right temple crashes into the hard rocky desert and he loses consciousness.

Liz Baker hated the desert. Hated most outdoors. Give her a good book, a window to see the view, and she'd be happy to leave the outdoors exactly where it is. But she fell in love with an outdoorsman. And love can sell itself well. It convinced her that Norm Baker was worth the compromise.

But that was five years ago. And the love had died. But she wasn't ready to throw away a five year investment. So here she was, out in Norm's beloved desert in this damn heat. They hadn't talked for the last half-hour. Not since she'd called him a self-centered prick who thought the whole world was out to get him. He turned back then, headed home and hadn't said a word since.

Liz reached into the cooler that sat between them and took out a bottle of ice-cold sparkling water. Just as she opened it, the SUV swerved and screeched to a halt, throwing her against the seat-belt and spilling the water all over her.

"What the hell are you doin', Norm?"

"Shit! I almost ran over somebody!"

"Are you crazy? There's nobody out there."

"Goddammit, go take a look if you don't believe me."

Liz unhooked her seat-belt, opened the door, and climbed down. She walked around to the rear and clamped her hand over her mouth in shock. A man lay face down on the side of the road. She looked back at Norm who was climbing down from the driver's side.

"We've got to do something."

"Do what? He's probably dead."

"You don't know that!" she screamed at him and she stepped, tentatively, towards the body on the ground. Kneeling down, she lifted his wrist and felt for a pulse.

"He's alive!"

"Barely, I'd say."

"But we can't just leave him here!"

"What do you expect we should do with him?"

"We've got to take him somewhere. To a hospital. A doctor."

"Damn it, Liz! There's no doctor or hospital for miles. You know that!"

"But we can't leave him."

Norm, thinking that he wished he'd never seen the man, now walked around the body, bent down and took a closer look. He moved the legs, looked at the upper body, saw the bruises and scratches on the side of the head.

"He's out cold. I don't see any serious injuries. But that's only a layman's opinion. He could still have a fractured skull."

"Can't we get him into the car?"

"Maybe. I'm not too happy about this. We don't know who he is. Or why he's lying out here in the middle of nowhere."

"Oh hell, Norm. He's a human being. We have no choice. I'll get some water."

She went back to the car. Norm decided he had no choice but to get the man out of here. So he opened the car door, thinking it lucky that he'd left the two rear seats at home. He grabbed a couple of large beach towels and spread them out. Then he went back and joined Liz who was bathing the man's eyes and sponging his lips with water. Still unconscious, they managed to lift him between them and carry him to the car where Norm scrambled inside and dragged him into the back. They laid him down and tucked up his knees so he would fit.

Fifteen

Indian Wells

Jim Sharkey woke in pain. He had a massive headache and every muscle in his body screamed in agony. He could see that he was lying in the back of a vehicle and the ride was a bumpy one. He managed to turn on his side and force himself into a sitting position.

"Hey, you woke up!" He looked up at the girl who had turned around in her seat and was smiling broadly at him, "We didn't know if you were gonna make it. Here, take this." And she handed him a bottle of water.

It was only then that he realized he was parched and his lips felt chapped and sunburnt. He pressed the bottle to his lips and gulped it down, thinking that it was the most precious drink he'd had in a long time. He remembered stumbling through the desert and falling. He remembered nothing after that.

"Where am I?"

"We're heading for LA. Found you lying out there in the desert. Unconscious. I'm Liz Baker. And my husband Norm," she pointed to the driver, who uttered a gruff 'hi' without even casting a glance over his shoulder.

"I sure owe you folks. I guess I could have died out there."

"That's a sure bet. Not much traffic out there. If we hadn't come along and picked you up, I doubt if you'd have survived. What the hell were you doing out there?"

"Oh, it's a long story."

"Seems to me that you had help getting out there. You just didn't hike out there in that gear!"

"I'm sorry. I know you must be curious. And you saved my life. That gives you a right to know. But I can't tell you what happened."

"Maybe we should take you to the nearest police station?"

"No, no, no! Absolutely not! What happened to me is very personal. I'll deal with it myself."

"OK! It's your call. We should drop you at a hospital or a clinic so you can get yourself checked out."

"No, I'll be OK. I'm only bruised and sunburnt. Where are we now?"

"Just passing through Indian Wells. We'll be in Palm Springs real soon."

"Drop me off in Palm Springs."

"Don't you want to stay with us till we reach LA?"

"No, I'd rather just chill out in Palm Springs for a day or two. Get my head cleared. Then I'll decide what to do. I think LA would be too much a shock to my system right now."

"Hey, if that's what you want to do … I'm just glad you're alive, that's all.

Jim thought about the note he'd received from Jack Miller before he left New York, the note that said *"then you can pick up your stuff in L.A. and live happily ever after."* Jack knew that he'd been screwed. Knew that Miller had taken the entire eight million. He just knew it. Miller had used him. Set him up. Anger began to build until he could only think of one thing. Revenge.

If it's the last thing I do I'll get the bastard. But I have to stay alive. Maybe I'm paranoid but it'll be safer to stay out of L.A. right now.

Sixteen

H-R (Himmler-Ramos) International's failure to consummate a major deal alerted them to their missing millions. When the funds did not arrive on time, the deal fell through. Carlos was livid. He blamed MetroBank for misdirecting or losing the funds. But he knew that the family did not want this to hit the newspapers. H-R treasured its low profile and if this went public, a Pandora's box might be opened. Carlos was certain of one thing: *This is the time for Cox to earn his money.* He picked up his cell phone.

MetroBank Vice President Walter Cox was H-R's relationship manager. Unknown to MetroBank, Cox was also in the employ of H-R, who paid him double his MetroBank salary to ensure that their interests were discretely looked after.

"Walter, we have a problem."

"Good morning, Carlos. What's the matter?"

Carlos described the deal that collapsed and the missing millions.

"You lost our money!"

"That's just impossible. Our International Money Transfer system is solid. Fully protected, fully encrypted. Can't happen. Did you check at your end. Maybe these monies were directed somewhere else. By mistake, of course."

"Do you think we're stupid or something? We checked. Our transfer instructions were correct."

"Just thought ..."

"Well, I don't give a shit what you thought, Walter! It fucking happened! That money never reached its destination."

"OK. I hear you. I'll examine our IMT transaction audit trail for that date. It will show where the funds went. Could take me a couple of days."

"No, I want to know by tomorrow. You have one day!"

With that, Carlos hung up.

Seventeen

Palm Springs

Jim Sharkey stood at the intersection of Frank Sinatra Drive and Bob Hope Boulevard. He'd never been here before and it all looked too rich for his blood. He crossed and walked until he reached the nearest gas station where he picked up a street map and a large bottle of water which he gulped down until he gagged. He went to the toilet and took stock of himself in the mirror. Reckoned he needed a change of clothes: shoes, socks, underwear, everything. But first he needed a drug store: something for his sunburn, shaving gear, Tylenol or stronger ...

And he needed somewhere to stay, somewhere where they wouldn't ask too many questions. But would there be such a place in Palm Springs. At least he still had cash in his wallet.

The kid pumping gas was only too happy to talk, almost as though people ignored him, treated him like a robotic extension of the gas pump. He told Sharkey that the Desert Lounge had cheap rooms to rent and it was near a shopping strip where he could find a drug store and anything else, including a McDonald's.

McDonald's, perfect, thought Sharkey, *a Big Mac will do me for dinner ...*

Tired and sore, he checked into the Desert Lounge forty-five minutes later. The room was basic, bed with tawdry comforter, cheap bedside lamp, flimsy furniture. He headed straight for the shower, dumped his clothes on the floor and stepped in. *Surprise, good shower, good pressure, a massage shower-head.* Stayed in for a long time soaking the desert out of his body. Then he toweled himself dry and went shopping.

First, he bought a newspaper and checked the latest. No mention of H-R's missing millions. No surprise in that but it's always nice to get confirmation, he thought. Next he bought a pay-as-you-go cell phone and then a bottle of Chilean red, with a screw top just in case the Desert Lounge had not provided a corkscrew for his cheap accommodation. Finally he picked up two big macs with extra large fries.

Back in his room, he moved the little table out from the corner and squeezed into the only soft chair in the place, found a glass in the bathroom, rinsed it out, screwed open the wine and filled the glass. He was ravenous. *A gourmet meal,* he joked cynically, as he wolfed down the two big macs and half of the bottle of red. Should be a beer, he thought, but reminded himself that, with the wine, he could imagine that the big macs were prime filet.

Sated, he sat back and let his mind take stock. When he woke up in the Mojave, he'd been angry and scared. Angry at himself for being such a fool, angry at Miller, angry at the conspirators in Caesar's, just plain fucking angry. More angry at himself. And scared too. Scared that he wouldn't make it out of the Mojave alive.

But now he looked coldly at it all. For the last two years he'd been playing the martyr, feeling defeated. He'd climbed so high and fallen so far, so fast, that it had almost destroyed him.

Yeah, this has been a wake-up call. That's for sure! He promised himself that he'd never again feel defeated. And he promised himself that he'd fight back.

He poured another glass of red and turned his attention to the dilemma he was in. He wanted revenge. He wanted to get Miller. And the millions? Decided he'd think about that when the time came. Getting Miller was more important than getting the millions. But where is Miller now? *That's the sixty-four thousand dollar question,* he intoned. He reckoned that the bank would not know that a couple of its International Money Transfers had been diverted. He'd used all the protocols, passwords, encryption. Nothing phony about his transfers.

If I'm right the cops and the feds will know nothing about this. Of course the Himmler-Ramos people might know now that their millions had gone missing. But, given the dubious nature of some of their relationships, he was sure they'd want no publicity. But, just like him, they'd want revenge. And they'd want their money back.

Miller must be the link! He almost screamed it out loud. *Why didn't I see that before?* Miller knew everything about H-R. And it only follows that H-R must know Miller. Would they suspect him? Would they make the connection? But how could they? There's no trace of Miller in this. *Only me!But if I'm right in thinking that I left no trace behind, then H-R does not know about me either. But I can't assume that. So I'll have to cover my tracks.*

I need to retrace my steps. I need to go back to Vegas. Miller set me up there and somebody might know where he is. But I need a car. I don't have enough cash to pick one off a used car lot. But I don't want my name on anything. Just as quick as he saw the problem, he also saw the solution. *Bill King! Dammit! Why didn't I think of Bill immediately?* They'd served in the Gulf War together. Afterwards Bill settled back in L.A., Universal City. He designed toupees for the stars and spent his weekends at the gambling tables in Vegas.

Eighteen

New York

Walter Cox swiveled his chair around and stared out of his twelfth floor window at the parade of yellow taxis moving north and south on Park Avenue. Normally a comforting sight to him, a rhythm confirming that all was well in his world. But not today. Today his stomach churned. It was only 11 am. Too early for his daily gin and tonic. He got up, left his office, and took the elevator to the ground floor. Out on Park, he turned right and headed north. He needed to think. And walking always helped.

The morning was clear, blue skies, and the street was crowded. Twenty and thirty-year olds, male and female, alone and in twos and threes, Wall Street attired, cell phone at the ear, snippets of conversation: *hedging, investment portfolios, the fed, yield curves, selling short ...* That was me, thirty years ago, Cox reminded himself. Driven by money. And the need to succeed. And power too. Power, the great aphrodisiac. Now I've got it, much of it by unorthodox means. My apartment on Central Park West, the house in the Hamptons. Has it all been a pyrrhic victory? *No, dammit!* He almost yelled out loud.

H-R had asked little of him. So he never felt compromised. But this call from Carlos was serious. He'd absorbed the shock of it by the time he reached 57th street. He turned back. And started to tackle it, one step at a time. As H-R relationship manager, he had full access to their accounts and business transactions. He intended to do a clinical examination of the money transfers of the day in question. But he must make it look casual, routine, raise no alarms. It would not do to trigger an internal audit.

He picked up his stride as he neared the bank. *Wonderful what a brisk walk will do for the mind,* he thought.

By 5 pm Walter Cox had examined the money transfer transaction log for the day in question and discovered that two H-R transfers, of two million each, had been made to the account of a Sam Smithberg at Citibank and two more, also of two million each, to the account of a William Johnson at Bank of America. He found that to be highly irregular. H-R had no history of significant banking relationships with Citibank or Bank of America customers in the US.

He picked up the phone and called Citibank. They confirmed that Mr. Smithberg had transferred the funds the same day he received it to a bank in the Cayman Islands. Bank of America also confirmed that the monies had been transferred out of the country. Not wishing to alarm either bank, he made them understand that his calls were part of his normal customer relationship duties and that he was fully satisfied.

He made the next call to Carlos and updated him on what he'd discovered. He could sense Carlos seething as he listened. But when he spoke, he sounded strangely cold.

"So there's no point in trying to identify who this Smithberg/Johnson is?"

"No. I managed to get customer descriptions from Citibank and Bank of America. I'd say it was the same person. But well disguised. I'll bet the cameras confirm that. But if we saw it we wouldn't learn a thing. Whoever it is does not look like Smithberg/Johnson. Of that I am certain!"

"Then you have to find out who made the transfer at your end."

"I did. They used a supervisory password. Few people have such access. I'll have to dig a lot deeper without raising any suspicions. I do not want to trigger an internal audit. You do not want to see H-R on the front page."

"You know what I want. Find me the bastard who did this. And find him soon. And don't fuck it up!"

The conversation ended. *The usual charming Carlos,* thought Cox.

Nineteen

Palm Springs

Jim Sharkey knew that Bill King's salon in Universal City was listed. A quick call to information on his cell phone and he had the number.

"Bill, how's life in the movie world?"

"Who is this?"

King's distinctive voice answered, with an undertone that he should know the caller but did not want to risk a guess.

"Jim Sharkey. I know, out of sight, out of mind."

"Aw, shit, Jimmy, you know I thought it was your voice but ...where are you?"

"Palm Springs"

"Palm Springs! What're you doin' there? I know, shacked up with somebody you shouldn't be with..."

"I wish, I wish. You'll never believe it."

Bill King could sense the gravity over the phone, a strain that wiped away the camaraderie and the levity.

"You're in trouble, aren't you?"

"That's an understatement. I need your help."

"OK, take my address and my cell number! "

Sharkey found a pen, jotted down the address and the number so that he could enter it into his cell phone when the call was over.

King continued, "Here's what I want you to do. Do you have enough money for a cab? You do, you do. Good. OK, take the next bus to LA. It'll take about 2 hours. Grab a cab in LA and take it to Sherman Oaks. I'll be here."

Sharkey reached Sherman Oaks by late afternoon. The taxi dropped him on the street outside King's house. He walked up to the front door and pressed the bell.

A lithesome blonde, California tanned, opened the door saying, "You must be Jim. I'm Lisa."

Sharkey wanted to hug her but reached out and shook her hand instead.

"Lisa, he didn't mention you."

"Ah, ha, he keeps all the best things secret!"

With that, King appeared, swept an arm around Lisa's waist and pulled her close, "Damn it, Sharks, it's great to see you. Come in, come in."

Sharkey stood back, in mock surprise, "You haven't aged a day. What's your secret?"

"Lisa keeps me young. Don't you, my love?"

Sharkey laughed loudly. King released Lisa and threw his arms around Sharkey, "It's been a long time, Jim."

They guided Jim through the house to the large redwood deck at the back. The coals were turning white on the barbecue and beer sat chilling in a barrel of ice.

"Wow!"

That's all that Sharkey could say. He hadn't expected this. King said,

"Listen up! After being dumped in the Mojave, we need to resuscitate you. What's your pleasure, beer or wine?"

"I'll start with a beer."

Lisa excused herself. King dunked his hand into the barrel, retrieved two beers, opened them, and handed one to Sharkey. They pulled up chairs and sat down. King opened a cigar box, picked up two cigars and offered one to Sharkey, who declined. Taking his time, he circumcised it, struck a match and slowly burned the end until it glowed. Halfway towards his mouth, he looked at Sharkey, expectantly.

"Guess you need to know what happened."

King twisted the cigar between his lips and nodded.

"I'll have to start a couple of months ago. In New York. My banking career had collapsed – that's a story for another day – and I was in the 'penalty box'. Sally moved out a year ago and took the kids. I'd hit bottom. That's when I met Jack Miller."

Sharkey told King everything that had happened up to being drugged in Caesar's and dumped in the Mojave. King listened without interruption. At the end he dug into the ice barrel and replaced their beers. Sharkey finished his first beer, took a gulp from the second, and looked at King:

"I got a wake-up call out there in the desert."

Not expecting King to respond, he continued:

"I'd become a loser. Lost my career. Sally left. Finished me. I hit the bottle hard. I'd reached a dead-end."

King interjected, " That's not my buddy, Sharks. The guy from the Gulf. Man, you were hot shit over there."

"Yeah, that guy died. I killed him. Until I woke up in the Mojave. Thought I'd die. For real this time. My whole life flashed through my head. And it was your buddy Sharks from the Gulf that saved me. He came back from the dead. Filled with the desire to live. And filled with the need for revenge."

Lisa picked that moment to appear again with three of the best looking steaks that Sharkey had seen in a long time. She placed them on the barbecue and asked Jim:

"How do you like your steak?"

"Medium rare would be perfect."

"That's for me. Bill likes his rare. Even better, raw."

Lisa's laughter gurgled deep in her throat as Bill raised his hands in protest.

The steaks turned out tender and delicious. *From dying of thirst in the desert to feasting like a king*, Jim Sharkey mused to himself. The conversation stayed light and frivolous during the meal, avoiding the reason that had brought him here. Bill King decided that Jim Sharkey's first order of business must be a good night's sleep.

Twenty

Asuncion, Paraguay

The Hawker Beechcraft King Air banked to the left north of Asuncion, levelled off, and eased down to 20,000 feet. Carlos Himmler-Ramos looked out at the Paraguay River below. The major artery of Paraguay, it was also the source of the Ramos dynasty. Strangely alien to him now. Since university he'd lived in Miami and the pastel shades of South Florida were now familiar to his eye and home to his heart.

He was alone on the flight. His brother, Eduardo, had been in Paraguay for the past month. Contrary to Carlos, Eduardo found Miami superficial and phony. Elena would never return to Paraguay. When she wasn't in Miami she was at home in New York, London, or Paris, or with her social circle on the Riviera.

In twenty minutes, the Beechcraft King Air would descend for a landing on the Himmler-Ramos private airstrip. A hard clay landing strip of about 3,500 feet, where turbo-props could easily land. The 9 passenger Beechcraft had been reconfigured into a luxury VIP shuttle for Carlos who was traveling alone.

The airstrip had been carved out of the 56,000 acres of the H-R estancion, the family homestead inherited from the

Ramos family, original founders of Paraguay. The original Ramos, also Carlos, had landed in 1537 with the Spanish expedition, headed by Juan de Salazar de Espinosa.

The family survived many wars and political battles over the next 400 years while amassing one of the largest fortunes in South America. But tragedy struck in 1940 when the entire family perished in a plane crash, leaving only one behind: their fifteen year-old daughter, Maria. She inherited it all. A guardian was appointed till she reached adulthood, a guardian who pursued his own interest instead of hers.

That's when a new immigrant came to her rescue. It was 1949 and she was 24. At 35 he was eleven years older but he was tall, handsome, charismatic and strong-willed. And Maria needed to acquire a strong-willed partner. Despite the efforts of the guardian to prevent it, Maria married Paul Himmler. A former member of the German SS, he had been smuggled into Paraguay by ODESSA, the organization of former SS members. ODESSA found it easy to shelter members in Paraguay, now run by General Alfredo Stroessner.

Six months after the wedding, the guardian's body floated to the bank of the Paraguay River; an unfortunate fishing accident. But fortunate for Paul Himmler who now assumed total control of all the Ramos holdings. Under Spanish naming customs, the first surname is traditionally the father's first surname and the second the mother's first surname. Paul Himmler wanted a stronger bonded name, one that would be carried by all descendants. So they became Himmler-Ramos. His son, Paul Himmler-Ramos II carried on the name to his children: Eduardo, Carlos, and Elena.

None of this passed through Carlos's mind as the plane's wheels hit the ground. He could only think of the inquisition that lay ahead.

"Señor Carlos, Señor Carlos!"

As he descended from the plane, he could see his driver standing close to the airstrip waving a huge panama hat and calling his name. The jeep stood waiting. He would be at the house in ten minutes.

Twenty-one

Sherman Oaks, California

Sharkey stopped running when he reached King's street. Checked his watch. 8:00am. He'd been running for twenty-five minutes. Back to basics, he'd told himself. He used to run every morning but, like everything else, he'd given that up too. But the new, angry Sharkey wanted that back. Running stimulated his mind and helped him solve the most difficult issues. At least that's what it used to do. Today his mind worked overtime. He realized that he needed more help. Bill King meant well but he knew that he needed serious intelligence. And he knew where to get it: Owen MacDara.

He had worked on the same team with Owen in their early careers at MetroBank. Owen was more ambitious. More willing to take risks. They had become close friends. Sally had once dated Owen. Briefly. Nothing serious. Owen was the first to congratulate them when they married. Owen had left MetroBank by then, successfully formed his own management consulting company, GMA Associates, and had prospered. He had wanted Jim to join him but, with a new baby in his family, Jim was afraid to take the risk. And Owen seemed to be surrounded by risk. At times of great national crisis, he'd been recruited by the President. Almost a spy, almost a lone wolf special agent. He had confided a little to Jim. Only a little. Curtailed by top secrecy and a reluctance to brag. Then tragedy struck. Owen lost his partner Kate and their baby son. Both died as Kate was giving birth. Jimmy shared morbid drunken evenings with Owen after that, the only way Owen knew how to deaden the pain of such loss. He still remembered the first drunken evening after Owen had visited their grave in Blauvelt and repeated, over and over again, what he had said to Kate as he stood at their grave: *Oh Kate, I loved you so much. I died inside when I lost you. And our son? What would he have been like? Oh, I don't mean what would he have looked like. I mean, what would he have been like inside. In his mind. In his soul. Half of you and half of me. More of you, if he'd been lucky. But it wasn't to be, Kate. And I must go on. So I came here to say goodbye.* And Owen did move on. He had already begun to devote all his time to his company. That anesthetized the wound and made him a very wealthy man.

By the time Jim's run had ended, he had resolved to call Owen and ask for help.

The aroma of coffee greeted him on return. And Lisa met him at the door, on her way out. Armed with a toasted bagel, cream cheese, and a large mug of coffee, he joined King.

King spoke first:

"Jim, I can help. I often go to Vegas on weekends to play poker. My addiction of choice. I knows Caesar's. I'm close with one of their managers."

"But this is my trouble, my fight. I only need a place to hide out for a day or two. And a sympathetic ear."

"Are you kidding me? I haven't had a challenge like this since the Gulf. And you've given it to me. And now you want to take it away again."

Sharkey laughed. It wasn't a laughing matter. But laughter was the only response.

"I should have known you wouldn't stay out of it."

"You're damn right. So let's take a look at this fine mess you've gotten yourself into. Who knows what?"

"That's it. I don't know. I'm sure that the H-R folks will find out that their money is missing and come after it."

"Come after who? Miller? You?"

"I don't know. I'm sure if MetroBank does a 'forensic' investigation they'll find my 'fingerprints' on it."

"But this H-R sounds like a shady enterprise. Maybe they won't want this to become public."

"You're right. They won't. So they'll use any means to get their money back. And silence anybody involved."

"If H-R doesn't ask MetroBank to investigate, how will they be able to trace it to you?"

"I don't know. But they'll have a way."

"And this Miller. What about him? How did he know about H-R and their multi-million dollar transactions? He must have had inside knowledge. Maybe he was the inside knowledge."

"At the time I didn't care how he knew. But you're right. If Miller knew a lot about H-R, maybe they know a lot about him."

"If that assumption is right, Miller will be high on the list of H-R's suspects. And they'll go after him."

"Miller set me up. Used me. And then dumped me, like garbage, in the desert. I want Miller and I need to get to him before H-R does."

"But you have no idea where he is?"

"Somebody knows. Somebody in Vegas was paid by him to take me out. I need to find that person. With a little persuasion, maybe they'll lead me to him."

"That's a big assumption…"

"But that's the last place I was. They'll probably think I'm dead, rotting out there in the desert. I need to find the girl who drugged me."

"OK. We'll take my jeep. I've got some equipment we may need. Meet me in the garage."

"I need to make a call before we leave. Can I use your phone? I want to call a good friend in Boston. I'd like him to look in on Sally. She knows nothing about this and she's expecting me to take the kids next weekend."

"Is that wise?"

"Yeah. Should have thought of it before now. We were colleagues – and friends – when we started our banking careers. Then he left and started his own company. Made a bundle. But he's had special assignments from the White House over the years. I don't know anything about it. Always thought he might have been in the CIA. I'll see if he can trace

Miller for me. He must have access to the right intelligence. And he and Sally were an item before she met me."

"Now I know it's not wise."

Sharkey laughed.

"I won't be long. I'll meet you in the garage in fifteen."

Twenty-two

Boston

Owen MacDara pulled his car into the sidewalk in front of the Residences at the Ritz-Carlton Towers, stepped out and handed his keys to the valet who greeted him with a huge smile, jumped in and drove the car away for safekeeping in the bowels of the hotel.

The doorman welcomed him into the residences lobby and he got into the private elevator, all marble and glass, a symbol of the luxury he'd surrounded himself with. He'd wanted this luxury. *I've earned it,* he told himself more often these days. But after only six months he felt as though he was in an *ivory tower,* one that had begun to isolate him from the real world.

Inside his apartment, he poured himself a malt whisky. Sipping it slowly, he crossed the living room, paused at the grand piano, and looked out at the Charles River and Cambridge. Dusk was setting in and the lights of the large CITGO sign illuminated Fenway Park. *Been a while since I've been to a Red Sox game*, he thought, *this writing business has taken over my life.*

The persistent ringing of his phone brought him out of his reverie. He crossed the living room to the bar and picked up the phone.

"Owen, I need your help!" the voice on the line pleaded, almost in panic. An unmistakable voice, even under stress. Jimmy Sharkey.

"Jimmy, is that you? What's the matter?"

"Long story, Owen, and I don't have much time. I'm in trouble and I need your help. Here's the short version of what happened."

For the next ten minutes Jim Sharkey described how he'd hit rock bottom, been seduced into relieving a company of its millions, screwed by Jack Miller, and dumped for dead in the Mojave desert.

"Jesus!"

That's all that Owen MacDara could say.

He and Jim Sharkey had been close colleagues and friends when Owen had been a senior executive at MetroBank. Owen had been an even closer friend of Jim's wife, Sally, before they married. Owen's peripatetic lifestyle was not for Sally and she had made her choice.

"Who did you steal the money from?"

"Agh, that too is a big problem. They are the H-R (Himmler-Ramos) company. The 'Himmler' founder was an escaped SS Officer who fled to Paraguay and was funded by ODESSA!"

Owen was stunned but Jimmy continued:

"I want you to look out for my family. If these bastards find out about me, who knows what might happen. I wouldn't put it past them to go after my family to get to me."

"Of course I will.   But we've got to rescue you. If this H-R company is what you think it is, and they find out about you …."

"Dammit! I know that. But I'm hoping they find out about Miller, not me."

"Where are you now?"

"LA. I'm with a good friend. A buddy from my days in the Gulf. We're heading back to Vegas."

"Back into the fire!"

"Yeah, I'm never going to run away again. I've stopped that."

"What are you planning to do?"

"Find the people who dumped me in the desert. I want revenge. And I want Miller. You can help me there."

"How?"

"Miller is probably not his real name. And if, as I now suspect, he was once involved in some way with the H-R company, then he must have left a trail. You have worked for the President. You must have sources. Find him for me, Owen."

"That's a big ask. How can I contact you?"

"You can't. I'll contact you."

Owen realized that he'd not kept up with the sources in Washington or Langley that would get him the information that Sharkey wanted on Roger Coleman. So he decided to contact the only person that he had kept in touch with; General Bartley Shields. He had first met Shields while he served in the US Army in Korea. Shields had been a Lt.

Colonel at Battalion HQ at Camp Red Cloud in Korea. Back in the States it hadn't take him long to make Colonel and then General. Major General Bartley Shields was very soon reassigned from the Army War College in Carlisle, Pennsylvania, to the office of the National Security Council to the President. And not long after his appointment to the National Security Council, he was named as the NSC special advisor to the President in all matters relating to terrorism. In that new capacity, General Shields reported directly to the President.

MacDara remembers enlisting the general's aid in combating a cult known as *The Circle of Sodom* They had infiltrated the Joint Chiefs and threatened to overthrow the US Government. Together they had saved the nation from a planned *coup d'état*.

He located the general's cell phone, called him and was immediately invited to the general's home in Alexandria, Virginia. He was retired now, had sold the big home in Essex, Connecticut, after his wife Millie had passed away two years ago. Moved to a smaller townhouse in Alexandria. Maintenance free and close to the Beltway. Near enough to keep a lifeline to the seat of power. *I'm sure it will sustain him*, thought Owen, *but first I must go to Sally.*

He packed an overnight bag, threw in a bunch of his toiletries from the bathroom shelves, grabbed his best boots and a couple of coats, and stashed everything in the hallway. He called the concierge to send someone up for his luggage and to bring his car around for him. That done, he was just in time to open the door for the young man who had come up for his luggage. He accompanied him down in the elevator and walked out to his waiting car.

Twenty-three

Sherman Oaks, California

King looked at Sharkey. "That's a long fifteen minutes."
Sharkey started to protest but King laughed "easy, Sharks,
easy. I'm just pulling your chain." And slapped him on the
back, "take a look at the equipment I'm bringing with us."

They moved to the rear of the car. King opened the trunk
and removed a black sports bag. He unzipped it and invited
Sharkey to examine the contents. He smiled as Sharkey
picked up one of the two Beretta M9s that lay in the bottom
of the bag. He held it as the memories flooded back. He
remembered the times that the pistol had saved his life in
close encounters with the enemy in the Gulf. Gently, he
replaced it in the sports bag and turned around to see King
facing him with a Heckler & Koch MP5 submachine gun in
his hands.

"Holy shit, Bill! Are we going to war?"

"Best to be prepared."

"Isn't this overkill?"

"You think? If they dumped you out in the Mojave to die,
they are capable of anything. We need to have the right
equipment."

"The M9s I can see. But the submachine gun?"

"It's my favorite. Indulge me. Besides, it's got a forty-round magazine and double the firing range of the Beretta. We might need this kinda power."

Conversation ended, King stored the 'equipment' back in the trunk and they left for Vegas.

Twenty-four

H-R Estancion, Paraguay.

Paul Himmler-Ramos II, a vital man, tall, stately, erect, leaned on the intricate carved head of a walking cane, looking out the window into the far distance. At sixty-two Carlos's father could easily be mistaken for a much younger man. It's in the genes, Carlos confirmed to himself, acknowledging that his grandfather, Paul Himmler, at 99, was still agile and mentally alert.

Eduardo lounged in a high-backed chair in the corner. A man he knew by video conference but had only met once sat at a large round oak table in the middle of the room. One hand rested on a stack of documents. Horst Richter, CEO of Himmler-Ramos International, with offices in London, Paris, Frankfurt and Zurich. His value to H-R was both professional and personal: he was a superb General Manager and his grandfather had been a member of ODESSA and a close friend of Paul Himmler, the H-R founder. As Carlos entered the room, he stood and clicked his heels.

His father turned away from the window, almost executing a perfect about-face using the walking stick for leverage. He said,

"We are waiting for an update."

Carlos could sense the tension in the room. He decided to stand while he briefed them, ending with his last conversation with Cox. His father asked,

"This Cox. Do you trust him?"

"Yes. We own him. If you mean, do I think he had any involvement in this theft? No, I do not."

"But what good is he? We're paying him to protect our interests at MetroBank – and to keep us informed of any threats, explicit or implicit. And now he's come up empty."

Horst Richter, fingers drumming steadily on the folder in front of him, could not contain himself:

"Carlos, this is not good enough! When these monies failed to reach our customer's account, a major deal fell through. They're threatening to sue us for losses that will make this theft puny in comparison. I have copies here of the contractual arrangements that depended on the timely receipt of those funds."

He drummed on the folder at his fingertips and continued,

"We have replaced the money and I am trying to repair the deal. It'll cost us but we need to keep H-R out of any adverse publicity, no matter what it takes to settle this."

He stood up, stretched his arms in front, brought his hands together, cracked his knuckles, and finally stood erect, at attention. No-one moved. They all watched him. Carefully.

He walked around the table until he was face to face with Carlos, and said,

"We want our money back …and we want blood. Do you understand?"

Twenty-five

H-R Estancion, Paraguay

The meeting had ended with Horst Richter's demand: *we want blood.* Recovery of the stolen millions was not enough. Those responsible had to pay. A lesson must be given, one that would deter anyone with similar intent. And all those with any association with the events leading up to, or following, this theft must also be terminated, with prejudice.

When tough decisions had to be executed, Carlos took responsibility. Taller than his brother and with a fairer complexion and Germanic looks, he displayed the Himmler genes. Eduardo was the opposite: shorter in stature, dark complexioned, dark eyed, with Hispanic good looks; he had the Ramos genes. He excelled at the financial management of the H-R company.

On the international side, all matters relating to the general management of H-R International fell to Horst Richter. All enforcement matters that crossed into the international arena also fell within Richter's gambit. At this time the theft seemed to be a US event and ownership went to Carlos.

Carlos had retired to his room when his cell phone rang. He could see from the caller identity that it was Walter Cox. All H-R phone calls, both personal and business, had end-to-end encryption, even more important now that it was known that the government were using a system called PRISM to spy on all phone calls. He answered the call:

"Carlos, I found him."

The excitement – and the anxiety – flowed through the phone from the voice of Walter Cox.

"Who did it?"

"One of our own, a former Senior VP. James Sharkey. He'd been laid off, given a year to find another job."

"So how did he do this? How did he breach your security?"

"He used a supervisory password to gain access to our International Money Transfer system. I do not know how he got that password. But he was very familiar with our IMT system."

"Goddammit, Walter, that's a major failure!"

"I know, I know. Sharkey's top security access had been removed months ago. If I report this to the bank, it will become public. There would be no way to prevent that."

"OK. Don't. We do not want H-R on page one. Where is this Sharkey now?"

"I don't know. But he is not the same man on the bank videos. The one who withdrew the money. Sharkey's height and body language is different. There's no match. Of course I'd like to get my hands on the actual videos but ...unless I stole them."

"Get them only if they can't trace it to you."

"We may not need them."

"Why?"

"I got one of our locksmiths to help me get access to Sharkey's apartment, with the excuse that we hadn't heard from him in a few days and we were concerned that something may have happened to him. "

"Why the hell didn't you tell me that in the first place?"

"Well, Sharkey wasn't there. The apartment was empty, sparsely furnished, the kind of place where you didn't intend to stay for long. I searched the place but saw nothing that would point me to Sharkey. Found a phone number for his ex-wife. Called her, pretending that I was a recruitment agency asking to speak to her husband. She said that he was seldom there and gave me his apartment and office phone numbers."

"Maybe she lied. I want to search that apartment. I'll have my people contact you today. Let them into the apartment."

"I'm not sure you should do that, Carlos"

"That's not an option."

Twenty-six

Cohasset, Massachusetts

"Uncle Owen!"
"Uncle Owen!"

As Owen MacDara stepped out of his car in Sally's driveway, eight-year old Ronan dashed into his arms and held on for dear life. Owen hugged him tightly and ruffled his blond curls affectionately, and then eased him to the ground. He could see Sally standing at the open door. Ronan held his hand tightly and pulled him up the driveway.

Up close, Sally did not disappoint the eyes. A natural blonde, slim and graceful with a body much younger than her forty-five years, she said nothing, simply smiled and took Owen into her arms. A full intense kiss on the lips resurrected memories of a time long past. Owen held her head back and looked into her eyes. Eyes that now seemed weary and tinged with sadness. She took Owen in one hand, Ronan in the other, and led them inside.

"Sarah's at her friend's house. Stayed over last night. But she'll be back for dinner."

"She must be all grown up now."

"Hah, she's fourteen and acting like she's twenty-one."

Owen laughed at that.

"Haven't seen her in almost three years."

"And whose fault is that?" chided Sally.

Owen didn't reply, simply threw up his hands in defeat.

Ronan ran off to fetch his latest games, hoping to ensnare Owen to himself for the evening. Sally led Owen out to the deck where two glasses and a decanted bottle of red stood waiting.

She poured and they clinked glasses, then sat overlooking the forest that bounded her large back yard. A single deer strutted, nonchalantly, out of the trees and across the lawn. For a moment life stood suspended. It seemed idyllic. But they couldn't postpone the reason that had brought Owen to her door.

"Where is he?"

"L.A. But he's on the move."

"What's going on, Owen? We've been very worried. Especially Ronan. He looks forward to those weekends with his dad."

"He's in a lot of trouble."

Owen described the phone call he'd received from Jim. He went on to detail, as much as he knew, about the mess he'd landed himself in, and Jim's insistence in pursuing the creep Miller who had him dumped to die in the Mojave. Sally sat incredulous. This was not the man she knew. *What happened to him? Did I cause that? But we couldn't make it work. We had no choice.* She stared into the trees that verged her back lawn. Trees that now looked ominous.

Owen saw the state she was in. He went to her, pulled her out of the chair, hugged her closely, wiped the tears from her cheeks with his finger. A finger that seemed to stray to her lips, traced the soft curve of her top lip, then her bottom lip. She trembled in his arms, and suddenly opened those lips and kissed him fully and deeply. He knew he shouldn't. But he kissed her deeply in return.

Then he pulled back, thinking that it would be so easy to fall in love again. *But I have nothing to offer and I don't want a ready-made family.* But, looking at Sally, he could see that she didn't understand.

"Sally, it's not what you're thinking."

"And what am I thinking, Owen?"

"That we can get back what we used to have."

Sally only shook her head, gently, from side to side as the tears welled up in her eyes. Owen continued.

"I'm not sure that I should move into your life now. And it would be so easy to do. We were never designed to be life partners. And we still aren't."

"Owen. I know, I know. But I just need a hug and a friend."

Owen drew her to him again and hugged her close.

Next morning he left for Alexandria, assuring Sally that he'd be back in a couple of days.

Twenty-seven

Bear Mountain, New York
The Huntsman Club

Set high in the New York hills, The Huntsman Club had a very select membership. As its name implied, it was a club for hunters: deer hunters, duck hunters, and all game hunters. Deep underground it housed an armory, storing all weapons under strict control. Another smaller, secret armory housed more deadly hunting weapons, ones used to hunt enemies who threatened the founders, their ethos, and their enterprises.

Beethoven's *Ninth Symphony* permeated the dining room. High ceilinged, tall windows framed by dark floor-length drapes, walnut paneled walls and two huge chandeliers made the room magnificent and imperious. Two waiters stood at attention, at the end of the room. It would not have been difficult to imagine that one had entered the Third Reich. It only needed swastikas on the tall drapes to complete the imagery.

At 6 pm, it was early for dinner. Only a few of the tables were occupied. The Pilkenroth twins, Hubert and Harvey sat at the corner table furthest from the entrance. They were already enjoying dinner: two 16oz sirloin steaks, Hubert's rare and Harvey's medium rare. Large Idaho baked potatoes, covered in sour cream and chives emitted faint steam because they had just arrived at table. As Harvey reached across for the mushrooms and onions, Hubert cut into his rare steak, savoring the blood seeping onto his plate. They were solid and square men, five seven in height, with round cherubic faces and piercingly blue eyes. One feature distinguished them: Hubert was bald and Harvey had an unruly mop of sandy hair. They were very wealthy, multi-millionaires, wealth self-made from their hedge fund and investment banking. But they had reached a plateau of risk. Losing or gaining millions failed to give them the surge of excitement that fuelled their days. They found that in their moonlighting work, work that suited their amoral and psychotic souls. Being grandchildren of ODESSA provided frequent opportunity for such soul satisfying work.

They ate in silence, occasionally smiling and nodding to each other as they gave each other mutual confirmation of their satisfaction. Sated, they leaned back in their chairs, closed their eyes, and let *Beethoven* assure them of their superiority. Simultaneously they opened their eyes, and sat up straight. Hubert said,

"Carlos said this one was urgent."

"But you know Carlos. Everything with him is urgent."

"Yeah, but we haven't had a gig in a while."

"Getting bored?"

"Damn right. Aren't you?"

"Yes. But he only wants us to search an apartment."

"Hey, who knows? Carlos's gigs are always good."

Ten minutes later they stood in their private armory, selecting their equipment of choice: a Walther P-38 for Hubert and a Browning P-35 High Power for Harvey. Within fifteen minutes, they drove out of the club's parking lot, and headed south towards New York. They had arranged to pick up Walter Cox at 61st and First Avenue, a quick exit and turnaround. They arrived fifteen minutes early and Walter Cox was already there, standing at the corner of First Avenue. He was a perfect match for the description they'd received from Carlos. Dark three-piece suit, well-shined black shoes, white shirt and conservative tie, lantern jawed and clean shaven, dark hair receding from forehead with an emerging bald spot. He carried an umbrella which he used as a walking stick. He could only be a banker.

They pulled into the curb, opened the passenger door and invited Cox into the passenger seat in front. Hubert sat directly behind him. Harvey drove. They turned back and took the 61st exit onto East River Drive heading south. Cox looked nervous. Harvey tried to settle him:

"Walter, you're a little twitchy."

"Carlos forced me into this."

"He's a hard man, our Carlos."

"I'm going to let you into Sharkey's apartment, that's all."

"Walter, Walter, easy now, that's all we need. You can toddle off somewhere as soon as you've let us into that apartment."

The apartment was on East 19th Street, in the lower east side of Manhattan. They drove south on the East River Drive and worked their way around until they reached their destination, the junction of Second Avenue and East 19th Street. They parked on the street close to Sharkey's building. Cox had an entry key to the outside door. They walked to the elevator in the rear of the run-down, poorly lighted entrance foyer. It was old, a little creaky, but still functional. They took the elevator to the seventh floor. Cox walked them to Sharkey's apartment and opened the door. Hubert and Harvey shouldered their way inside. Cox followed but the twins stopped, turned around and looked at him.

Hubert spoke, "Walter, we'll take it from here."

Walter Cox offered no protest. He felt relief. He did not want to spend another minute in the company of the twins. He backed out of the apartment and left.

Hubert and Harvey slipped on surgical gloves and Harvey put a shower cap over his hair; no point in leaving DNA around. A quick glance confirmed that the apartment was indeed Spartan. Railroad style, with bathroom, small single bedroom and equally small kitchen leading off the hallway to the left. The hallway ended in one large living/dining area. Dark wall coverings and dim lighting made the place feel like a cave.

The small dining table had been pushed into a corner. A large couch backed up against one wall and a wide screen TV adorned the opposite wall. An old office desk nestled at the end wall, under the only window in the apartment. An old scuffed office chair sat uncomfortably in front of a dust covered Dell desktop computer.

Harvey said, "I'll take the computer."

Hubert laughed, "Bet you won't find any porn."

Harvey grimaced and threw a punch at Hubert who stepped out of range. Frivolity over, they both set about the serious business of discovery. Hubert started with the bathroom, searching the medicine cabinet, looking under the mats, taking everything out of the small garbage bin and examining each item meticulously. He used the same rigorous approach in the bedroom, searching under the mattress, behind pictures and every possible place of concealment. In the kitchen he opened every tin on the shelves and dumped the contents out, merging tea, rice, coffee, sugar and couscous into an unwholesome recipe. Finished, he joined Harvey in the living room, declaring:

"Nothing."

"Nothing on this system either. Hardly ever used it."

"This guy had no life. There's no evidence of it."

"Maybe, maybe not."

"What do you mean?"

"I found a scrap of paper under the keyboard with a name and address on it. Jack Miller. An apartment on West End Avenue. May be nothing. Probably a computer repairman or something."

"Can't make assumptions, Harvey. We'll check it out."

Twenty-eight

West End Avenue,
New York

Hubert and Harvey pressed the bell at the door of the apartment that they had found on the piece of paper in Sharkey's apartment. They waited a few minutes, no answer, so they pressed the bell again. Finally, they heard the door being unlocked. It opened and a good looking young woman greeted them in a seductive foreign accent, with an annoyed look on her face:

"I am not buying!"

"And we're not selling. We'd like to speak to Jack Miller," said Harvey.

"Jack is not here."

"Where is he?"

"Who are you?"

"Friends."

"I don't believe you."

Hubert looked around, saw that there was no-one on the floor, grabbed the young woman, placed a hand over her mouth and forced her into the apartment. Harvey closed the door behind them. Hubert released her and she ran, to the phone, picked it up and yelled:

"I am going to call the police."

"No, you are not," said Harvey, who pulled the phone out of her hands. She backed away, pretended to give up, then made a mad dash around them for the front door. Hubert stopped her. Harvey joined them and they each took an arm and dragged her to an upright chair where Harvey held her and Hubert talked:

"What is your name?"

"Inga," she sobbed, her eyes red-rimmed and scared.

"Tell us what we need to know and we'll leave."

But Inga just sobbed uncontrollably and tried to wrench her arms away from Harvey, to no avail.

"Tell us where Jack Miller is."

Inga knew she could not hold out any longer. Besides, she really didn't owe Jack this kind of loyalty. Sure, he'd been good to her, gave her this place to stay, never asked any questions, but she never pledged to keep her mouth shut about anything. And she hoped these two crazy twin looking men would let her go if she told them what they wanted to know.

"He left a few days ago. Left with a friend of his."

"What was the friend's name?"

"Jim Sharkey"

"And where did they go Inga,"

"They went to Las Vegas."

"Where in Las Vegas?"

"Caesar's Palace, I think. That's all I know."

Hubert exchanged a knowing glance with Harvey. They both agreed that this was most likely all that Inga knew. So Harvey held both of her arms tight behind the chair with his right arm as he put his left arm around her neck and squeezed. Her eyes bulged out of her head, whimpers bubbled from her lips, saliva trickled down her chin. Harvey squeezed tighter and gave her neck a final twist. She suddenly relaxed in his arms. He released her and she slid to the floor. He knelt and checked her pulse. None. She was gone. He knew they had no choice. They could not leave her alive to identify them. But it gave him a thrill. Life had just become less boring.

Efficiency was the twins' middle name. They donned their surgical gloves. Harvey already had his hair covered neatly by a black beret. His black head oddly now matched Hubert's totally bald head. They wiped anywhere that they might have left fingerprints. They had not moved around the apartment so they gave the door and the chair a thorough cleaning. Then they examined Inga's body to ensure that nothing of them showed on her, especially skin detritus from Harvey's arms that might have adhered to her. They cleaned her exposed throat and wrist areas thoroughly. Satisfied they turned their attention to the rest of the apartment. They had gotten what they had come for, the whereabouts of Jim Sharkey and a bonus, the whereabouts of the mysterious Jack Miller. At least they had their last destination. Caesar's Palace in Las Vegas. But they still searched the apartment. It was much more upmarket than Sharkey's apartment but still Spartan. Basic furniture, minimal food in the refrigerator, no books or magazines in sight. But they did find a digital camera, most probably Inga's. They opened it and viewed the photos. Mostly touristy type pictures of New York, except for a couple that showed Inga and a tall, distinguished looking man posed together outside the United Nations. Could be that they were looking at Jack Miller. That would be an added bonus. They'd email them to Carlos right away.

They had booked into the Waldorf for the night and, as soon as they checked in to their room, they loaded Inga's photos on to their laptop and emailed them to Carlos. Using their encrypted cell, they called him (Harvey elected to be the communicator), and before he could say anything, Carlos said:

"I want an update on New York. Now."

"OK. I'll put us on the speaker."

Hubert and Harvey proceeded with a detail report on Jim Sharkey's apartment, the discovery of the Jack Miller address, Inga and her 'persuaded' revelation that Miller and Sharkey had gone to Vegas, and the unfortunate, but necessary, end to Inga. They assured Carlos that they had left no evidence behind but they did agree it would be better if Carlos sent in the 'cleaners'. Finally, Harvey asked:

"Did you get the photo we emailed of Inga and that guy. We thought it might be Miller."

"Yes, I got it. But it's not Miller."

"Oh well, it was worth a shot."

"I know who it is. He may have called himself Miller but, when I knew him, he was Coleman. Roger Coleman."

"You know him."

"He's a conman. Used to work for our company. Wheedled his way into our family. Our sister, Elena, was going to marry the bastard. Until we found out that he was not Roger Coleman. He stole that name. And he's not Miller. That's another phony name."

"Well, who is he?"

"That we will find out. He is behind the theft. I got the videos from Cox. The ones at the banks when he was moving our money. It's him. He was using a disguise but there is no mistake. Guess he used Sharkey to get into Metro's international money transfer system."

"What do you want us to do?"

"Go to Vegas now. Find Coleman and this Sharkey. Get rid of Sharkey. But I want Coleman alive. Do you hear me? I want him alive. And there's a loose end I want you to clear up in New York. He knows too much and he has outlived his usefulness."

"You don't mean .."

"Yes I do. Getting you into Sharkey's apartment and getting these videos are his last assignments. Take care of it. Cleanly."

As Harvey and Hubert were about to hang up, Carlos said, "I might see you in Vegas. I want this bastard so much."

Twenty-nine

Hubert and Harvey Pilkenroth drove upstate to their mansion, nestled in the New York mountains. Harvey pushed a button on his remote and the large doors at the end of the driveway swung open, making the walls on either side seem higher. The driveway stretched ahead, bordered by tall Italian Cypress trees on one side and illuminated by strategically placed lighting on the other side. Soon the house itself came into view. The ante-bellum façade hid a most modern building, one that had taken advantage of every innovation in contemporary construction, from solar to heat exchange systems, from passive to underfloor heating, from waste composting to rainwater recycling. Truly 'off the grid'. It's not so much that the twins were concerned about the earth's scarce resources. It was more about their need to be independent of the system.

Harvey hit the remote again and one of three contiguous garages swung open. Hubert drove the Mercedes-Benz SUV inside. As the door to the inner hallway opened, the garage door automatically closed behind them. For the time being, they left their weapons in the SUV. They'd be driving to Teterboro Airport in the morning to fly to Las Vegas. They kept their own Bombardier at the airport. Hubert was an accomplished former navy pilot.

They walked through till they reached the large central hallway. They were alone in the house. Their caretaker and their cook had already left for the evening. They had their own home provided for them on the estate.

They climbed the staircase to their own bedrooms. Sated by the dinner at the club they decided to go to their matching bathrooms, take steam showers and sit in their Jacuzzis. They probably wouldn't see each other until breakfast in the morning.

Harvey bunched two large pillows on his king size bed, turned on the reading light and picked up the book he'd been reading: Barry Eisler's *Graveyard of Memories,* the story of his Japanese-American assassin, John Rain. Harvey considered Rain to be a 'fellow-traveler'. He thought of himself as a noble assassin. Photographs hung on the wall near him. A fading one of his father. A grand, imperious one of his mother. And one of two little boys, side by side, mischievous smirks on their faces. Twins in almost every way. He closed the book again and lay back on the pillows to unearth his own *graveyard of memories.*

They had lived in an old red brick house in a Queens neighborhood in New York. Not wealthy but not poor either. Their father sold things. They never knew what. But he was always 'on the road'. A traveling salesman, they supposed. He was seldom home. Their mother was a charity organizer, a 'do-gooder', a social gadfly who challenged all the society norms. The twins were often left alone. Harvey chuckled at that thought. Left alone because they terrified all their childminders. At ten years old they reveled in acts of disobedience and disorder. At high school they had graduated to acts of violence: killing all the cats on their street and leaving each in a place that added to the trauma: inside the door of the church, in the meat aisle in the supermarket. They were never caught. Or even suspected. To their neighbors, they were boys to be admired: two perfect twins, growing up well, despite their dysfunctional and often missing parents.

But life changed for them at fourteen. Their mother collapsed and died of a brain hemorrhage. Their father had not been seen for over a year and did not return for the funeral. The boys were sent to live with their uncle Hans, a man who was a total stranger to them. Hans Pilkenroth lived in the house that had once sat on the land where their own new house now stood. He was in his sixties, single, wealthy, odd. He was focused on two things: education and heritage. Each boy had his own room, fully equipped with desk, computer, Internet, and the latest technology. A library filled with classics and modern literature (but completely devoid of poetry) faced them when they ascended the stairs. Two shelves held volumes that covered (and praised) the Third Reich. One shelf held only books by and about Adolph Hitler: *Mein Kampf*, Hitler's autobiographical manifesto; *Adolph Hitler a Picture Book Series; Adolf Hitler Speaks Series; Adolf Hitler War Speeches*; and more. On the second shelf, books about the SS took prominence: *The SS Calls You; SS Song Book; SS Leadership Guide; SS Ideology; SS Chronicles; SS Heroes.* Books by Dr. Joseph Goebbels, Hermann Goering, Rudolf Hess, Heinrich Himmler, Joachim von Ribbentrop, and others completed the shelf. And so Hans started to educate Harvey and Hubert on their Nazi heritage. Weekly, on the firing range in a remote area of his property, he taught them their skill in weapons.

By the time they were admitted to Vanderbilt University in Tennessee (funded by Hans) their raison d'être had been fully formed. In their years at Vanderbilt they excelled in finance and, with seed money from Hans, had begun their own financial trading. An enterprise that would lead to their own hedge fund and their elevation to their multi-million standing at the early age of twenty-six.

In the latter years at Vanderbilt, Hubert learned to fly at a local private flying club. Leaving Harvey to execute their trades, he satisfied that passion by joining the navy and learning to fly at NAS (Naval Air Station) Pensacola, Florida. He had further 'on the job' training from TOPGUN graduates. Back in civilian life, he helped Harvey grow the profits from their hedge fund into the billions. His first indulgence was the purchase of their own Bombardier aircraft.

In their years at Vanderbilt they continued to feed their need for 'blood' by terminating the occasional vagrant and drunk they encountered in Nashville. The authorities were troubled by the increase in random killings but no perpetrators were ever found.

Their uncle Hans had them inducted into the secret international 'descendants of ODESSA.' There they would find plenty of opportunities to satisfy their 'blood lust'. In their late twenties, their uncle Hans passed away and left them his property. They immediately designed and built the house they lived in today. They stayed single. They had no partners in life. Hubert bought and paid for affairs with many beautiful, and prominent women. Just like his passion for 'blood' those affairs satisfied his passion for sex. Harvey had no liaisons. He was almost asexual.

The noise woke Harvey. He had fallen asleep in his sojourn through his own *graveyard of memories* and his book had slid off the bed on to the floor. He picked it up, closed it, and turned off the light. Sinking into the pillow, he fell asleep again thinking about how much he was looking forward to Las Vegas.

Thirty

Alexandria, Virginia

General Bartley Shields was looking forward to Owen MacDara's arrival. His days were pleasant but predictable. Owen would break that. Eleven a.m. Coffee time. Owen was due by noon.

He took his coffee and moved out of the kitchen into his front sitting room. Sipping the coffee, he reminisced. He thought again about the first time he had met MacDara in Korea. Used to call him the FBI—Foreign Born Irish! Tried to keep him in the Service. But MacDara had wanted to go back to New York and make a million. And he did. Many millions. MacDara just wanted to do his two year hitch and get out. Tops at everything. Earned the top marksmanship badge for his accuracy with the rifle. And then there was the karate. MacDara wanted to understand the people, the Koreans. So he started taking lessons in the Korean language. When Karate classes started, he was one of the first to sign up. Many dropped out, but not MacDara. In a few months he had a brown belt and was well on his way to a black belt, as best as I can remember, Shields recalled.

But those are very early memories, he thought, *my most vivid memories are the ones minted in blood; MacDara's life or death struggle to save this nation from those who would destroy it.* Then he caught himself and laughed. *If MacDara heard me say anything like that, he'd walk out. But, as corny as it sounds to me, it's exactly what I believe.*

Punctuality being a discipline he lived by, Owen arrived at the general's house at exactly twelve noon. General Shields opened the door and they stood looking at each other, assessing the change the years had brought. Owen thought that the general still carried himself as he remembered: erect, square shouldered, fit, topped by a crown of white hair, not cut in a military style any more. General Shields could see little change in Owen: tall, trim, still the Irish face with the smiling eyes.

"Owen, you haven't aged a day!"

"Well, I just hope that I look as good as you do at your age, Sir."

"Come in, come in, flattery doesn't suit you."

General Shields ushered Owen through the house into the open kitchen dining room. The table was set for two. A large platter of cold cuts sat in the middle: cheese, prosciutto, lettuce, tomatoes, fruit.

"Lunch time," the general announced.

"I didn't expect you to feed me."

"But I must. Don't you remember? The first time we met was over the table at the New York Yacht Club."

Owen remembered that day as though it was yesterday. He remembered that the food had been good; his scallops were the best and he could still see the General nod his approval of his blackened Cajun-style salmon.

"Oh I do remember. As though it were yesterday."

"Sit, sit," commanded the General as he reached for the Chablis and filled their glasses, "won't be as good as Millie's."

Owen could see that the general needed to talk about his late wife. Owen remembered his visit to their home in Essex and the meal. Millie Shields, renowned among the Washington wives for her skill in the kitchen, had prepared a vegetarian goulash with wild rice followed by her special dessert of pears in red wine sauce. Owen could still imagine the jig that his taste buds performed.

"Yes, I do remember a wonderful meal she prepared at your home in Essex. She was a special lady."

"Two years now. They say that time heals but, believe me, she's as fresh in my memory as ever. I almost expect her to walk in any minute."

The general's eyes were a little moist but a happy smile framed his countenance.

Lunch and small talk over, they retired to the sitting room.

"I take it you need my help," probed the general.

"I do. Don't worry. I'm not bringing another threat to the nation to your doorstep!"

"Now I'm really disappointed to hear that," joked Shields.

Owen laughed, "I'm sure this nation is always under threat. If I were President I doubt if I could sleep at night."

"So what brings you to my door?"

Owen knew that he had to brief the general thoroughly on the trouble that his friend, Jim Sharkey, had got himself into. So he described, word for word, every detail of the phone call he had received from Sharkey. And his reason for being here: find out who Roger Coleman/Jack Miller really is and where he is now. General Shields grew more sombre as the story unfolded. His body language exhibited a distaste for it all.

"But Sharkey is a felon! We don't protect felons, even if they are friends."

"But, General …"

"Call me Bart. I'm not sitting in the West Wing now."

"OK. Sharkey's life is in great danger. They've already tried to kill him by dumping him in the Mojave. And he believes strongly that these crazy twins might go after his family."

"Still, these are murky waters, Owen."

"Come on, Bart. Jim Sharkey is not a criminal. He's a failed banker."

"These days that's an even worse claim. Bankers are not held in very high esteem at the moment."

"But we could almost say that Sharkey was liberating ill-gotten gains."

The general looked at Owen, waiting for him to elaborate, to defend his statement. And he did,

"Bart, the people who are out to kill him are operatives working for the Himmler-Ramos company, a conglomerate headquartered in Asuncion, Paraguay. A company founded by an escaped SS Officer, Paul Himmler. Obviously funded by

ODESSA. Who knows what monies they launder? Who knows what banned organizations they fund?"

"That's high speculation. You have no proof of this."

"No, I can't prove it. But you know I'm right. I know you do."

"OK. Suppose I accept that you are right. And suppose I go a step further and assume that you can provide the proof. What do you want me to do?"

"Use your intelligence network. As I said, find out who this Roger Coleman is …and where he is now."

"I don't see how this knowledge will help things."

"The H-R thugs are on Coleman's tail right now. Sharkey wants to get to him before they do. He wants closure."

"Closure?"

"Whatever it takes, short of announcing himself to the public. He assumes that H-R thinks he died in the Mojave. He believes that Coleman contracted to have him killed. So he assumes that Coleman thinks he's dead too."

"So why doesn't he drop the entire thing?"

"Ah, he thinks that they'll find out that he's alive. And he wants revenge."

"And that will probably get him killed."

"Yes, I know. But if I put myself in his shoes, I'd probably be doing what he's doing."

"It's a mess."

"I know. But he's a good friend. And I'm asking you to do this for me. Not for him. For me, for old time's sake."

"Damn it, Owen. You are a good salesman. I had forgotten that skill of yours."

Nothing more to say. General Shields assured Owen MacDara that he would tap his network for the information. Owen promised to visit from time to time. And not to bring any more problems to the general's door. As he left, he almost felt that Bart Shields had an urge to hug him.

Thirty-one

Teterboro Airport
New Jersey

"Vegas! I love Vegas," said Harvey to himself.

Hubert laughed out loud and nodded his head. They had reached Teterboro Airport in New Jersey, a short thirty minutes from Manhattan. Their own private jet was fuelled and ready to go. They'd already filed their flight plan to Las Vegas Airport. Their Bombardier did about 500 mph so they'd be on the ground in Vegas in a little under five hours. Hubert would pilot. He'd spent four years as a Navy pilot and he'd enjoyed every minute of it. Harvey considered himself co-pilot but did not have the flying experience or passion for the air that Hubert did. He doubted that he'd be capable of taking over should anything happen to Hubert. So every time that they flew – and that was often – he lived with that concern.

Once they were in the air Harvey relaxed and said, "Must be three or four months since we were in Vegas."

"Five months exactly," said Hubert.

"I didn't think it was that long."

"Kinda miss it, don't you."

"Yeah, I'm itching to hit the tables in Caesars."

"First things first. We need to take care of Carlos's problem before we do any gambling."

"An appetizer! It'll just whet our appetite."

They both started to laugh, in unison, like they did so often at their own jokes. A macabre sense of humor, all their own.

Thirty-two

Caesar's Palace, Las Vegas

Hubert and Harvey smiled as the terminal flashed VIP when their reservation hit the screen at the check-in at Caesars. Big gamblers. And big gamblers they were. Harvey's favorite game was *chemin de fer*. He had won and lost thousands at it. Well known at Caesars, they were greeted enthusiastically.

"Please tell Dave Pollock that we're here and we'd like to see him."

"Yes, sir, Mr. Pilkenroth, we'll contact him immediately", the clerk gulped, knowing the twins reputation as generous tippers, "we have your usual room ready for you. Simon will take your bags."

A welcome note and a bottle of their choice red from the Columbia Valley awaited them. They tipped Simon and Harvey uncorked the wine and poured two glasses. Raising his own, he clinked Hubert's, saying "here's to the fun and games."

The phone rang and Hubert picked it up.

"Hi Dave."

"Yes, good to be here."

"No, it's been about five months. Too long."

"That's funny! I'm sure they'll still remember us at the tables."

Preliminaries aside, Hubert got right to the point.

"Dave, we need to see you. It's very important."

Dave Pollock was mystified. Hubert's voice had an edge to it. What do they need from me, he wondered? Everything was already provided for them. Even though they hadn't been to the tables for a while, they were big spenders when they did come. And their credit was impeccable. Figured he'd better see them right away.

The twins greeted him, standing side by side, as he entered their suite. Hubert offered him a glass of wine but he declined. They guided him to a table, surrounded by four comfortable chairs, nestled in the curve of a bay window that looked out on the Vegas spectacle below. Hubert spoke:

"We're looking for someone."

"How can I help?"

"We are sure he was a guest here recently. Possibly accompanied by another man."

"Why do you need to find him?"

"It's a family matter. He's the fiancée of a young lady, a member of our extended family. They were planning their wedding when he simply disappeared a few weeks ago. She is distraught. There was no sign of any problems. We have information that he came here to Vegas, to Caesars."

"Didn't anyone try to contact him?"

"Absolutely! Reservations say they have no record of him. He could have been using one of two names, Roger Coleman or Jack Miller."

"I'm sure reservations are telling you the truth. Was he a gambler?"

"Yes, that's his weakness. Big time!"

"Maybe he stayed somewhere else. And if he got in too deep, he could be in real trouble. If he owed the mob, maybe you should call the police on this one."

Harvey almost jumped out of his chair, "No cops, Dave. We don't want to see the family on any florid scandal sheets!"

"Then the man you want to see is Bruce Morgan. If anything bad went down he'll either know about it – or have been involved in it. But you better be careful. He can be bad for your health."

They both laughed at that. A joint laugh, the same cavernous, sinister sound to both. Dave had never experienced them like this before.

"He might have been travelling with another man. A heavy gambler too, we believe. His name is James Sharkey. Can you let us know if he stayed here?"

They had nothing more to say and Dave was in no mood to prolong the visit. He left, ran Sharkey's name through the register and discovered that he had checked in, alone, for one night about two weeks ago. No-one remembered him. It was as though he had never existed. Dave phoned the twins and told them.

Thirty-three

LA to Vegas

Forty minutes after leaving Sherman Oaks, King and Sharkey took the exit onto I-15, the N/Ontario Freeway which would take them all the way to Vegas. King was big into country music. Sharkey could take it or leave it. But it was King's car and he didn't ask permission. They would be crossing desolate, open desert so whatever it took to stay alert. They had exhausted all their conversation and they expected trouble in Vegas. Better to listen to country than dwell on the trouble ahead. The 300 mile trip from LA to Vegas should take about four hours but King said there were times that traffic got so bad that it had taken him up to seven hours. When they reached Barstow they'd be half-way there and they reckoned that they'd rest and grab lunch somewhere.

They made good time and reached Barstow in about two hours. Barstow had lots of gas stations and fast food joints. They filled up and settled for a diner.

Burgers were the big item on the menu so they both ordered the same. Fat, juicy, sitting in a huge seeded bun, surrounded by the best french fries he reckoned he'd ever seen, Jim Sharkey thought he was in heaven. Mouths full they tried to speak but gave up until they could. Finally, Jim spoke,

"This Pollock. Can you trust him?"

"Yea, he's a good friend."

"But good friends don't always look out for your back."

"Ah, ha, but I have a *little black book* on this good friend."

"But if he's only helping us because of that …"

"He's not. I'd never need that leverage. Believe me."

"Ok, I've been screwed too often lately, that's all."

"Sharks, listen, I know that. Ease up."

Sharkey knew that he was up tight, knew that he had to relax, knew that he was a lucky man because he realized that he could be rotting out in the Mojave now. So he relaxed and started to laugh, at himself. Car and bodies fuelled, they hit the road again. Bill King had stashed a hamper in the car, filled with bottles of ice cold water – the other fuel their bodies needed to stay hydrated in the 113 degree temperature of the Nevada desert. *Viva Las Vegas* by Elvis flowed from the car's speakers as they passed through Baker. They had covered two-thirds of their journey and it seemed that no time had passed when they reached Primm, which told them that Vegas was forty-five minutes away.

They took exit 38 for Flamingo Road and avoided Las Vegas Boulevard (the Strip). They took Dean Martin/Industrial to the west and soon arrived at Heidi's, a small café off the Strip. Bill King had called ahead and Dave Pollock was waiting for them. Dave was a large, jolly looking man, jowly and balding with big warm eyes and an inviting face. He saw Bill as they entered and rose immediately.

"King, you old dog," he gripped Bill with both hands and looked inquisitively at Sharkey.

"Dave, this is Jim Sharkey. A good friend. And an old buddy from the Gulf."

"Jim, good to meet ya…thanks for your service."

"You never thanked me," protested Bill.

"Ah, cut the shit, we're old friends," said Dave, with a loud hearty burst of laughter.

They joined Dave at his table and ordered three tall coffees from the waitress. A sudden realization dawned on Dave Pollock. He looked at Jim and said:

"Did you say your name was Sharkey? James Sharkey?"

"Yep, but nobody calls me James. Jim or Jimmy is fine. Bill calls me Sharks."

King laughed out loud at that.

"So, what's this all about?" asked Dave.

"You'd better tell the story," said Bill to Jim.

Sharkey and King had already decided that the theft of H-R's millions had to remain secret. So Sharkey had invented a new backstory: Miller and he had agreed to meet in Vegas to celebrate an investment deal that was about to make them very rich. If anything happened to one of them, the remaining partner would get the entire proceeds of the deal: $4 million dollars! He told the story verbatim from the time he arrived in

Las Vegas, not skipping a thing until he woke up in the Mojave desert.

Pollock sat, transfixed.

Then he looked directly at Sharkey and said, "That's not the story I just heard."

Now it was Sharkey and King's turn to be astonished. They said nothing, waiting for Pollock to explain himself.

He asked Jim, "Do you know the Pilkenroth twins, Hubert and Harvey?"

"Never heard of them," answered Jim.

"Well, they've heard of you. They're weird and they're filthy rich. Come here to gamble from time to time. Arrived this morning and asked to see me. Said they were tracing a guy who was engaged to marry a young lady, a member of their extended family. Said he was a heavy gambler and had disappeared a couple of weeks ago. Said he'd left his fiancée distraught. Maintained that they had information that he'd come to Vegas. To Caesars. Gave me two names for the guy. Said he could be using the name Jack Miller—or his own name, Roger Coleman. And they said he might have been travelling with another big gambler called James Sharkey."

Sharkey was now thinking fast. He knew he had to fit his story into the one that Pollock had just told him.

"God damn! Miller was a crook, a con man that's for sure. He never met me here to close the deal we were working on. But he must have closed it and decided not to share it. That's why he tried to get rid of me. But I never heard the name Roger Coleman. And I know nothing about any impending marriage of Millers. And I never heard of these twins. I don't know who they are!"

"Well, they know about you."

"So what did you tell them?"

"Nothing. There was nothing to tell them. According to our records Sharkey had stayed only one night. And nobody remembers him. Told them that it was as though he never existed."

"So that's it then."

"No, that's not it. They won't give up."

Pollock sat silent and unsmiling. Looking directly into Sharkey's eyes, he said:

"I can find that girl for you. The one who drugged you."

"If I can get her to talk, maybe I'll find out who was behind it."

"OK, I can get the videos of that night. We can see who entered and left the floor at the time you were there. Do you think you would recognize her?"

"Her face is burned into my brain."

Thirty-four

Caesar's Palace

Sharkey and King sat in Pollock's office in Caesar's Palace watching him start the video of the night in question. Starting at five pm the video showed all access, elevators and stairways, to the Fantasy Suite floor. Punctuated by long periods of empty views, the elevators would open and a single person, or a couple, or a laughing group of four or five, would emerge. At times, others would arrive and wait for a down elevator.

"Wait. Hold that," said Sharkey, as a young woman emerged from the elevator. Pollock paused the video, froze it at the exact frame and zoomed in for a better view.

"No, that's not her," said Sharkey.

At exactly 7 pm on the video another young lady exited the elevator.

Once again Sharkey said, "Hold it."

Pollock froze it and zoomed in on her face. Immediately Sharkey stood up, animated:

"That's her! That's definitely the one who drugged me. Who is she?"

Pollock captured the image, transferred it to disk, and offloaded it to a thumb drive.

"OK, let's roll it. I want to see the next hour's footage," said Sharkey.

Pollock continued the video and they watched the traffic to and from the floor. Nothing of interest until they saw the girl who drugged him catch the down elevator. Dave paused the video again and looked at Sharkey, who said:

"Let it roll. I'm lying unconscious in the room now. They'll need to get me out of there soon."

So they continued to watch the video. Twenty minutes later two guys, in hooded track suits, pushed a large trunk, on wheels, on to the down elevator.

"Stop it," said Sharkey.

Dave Pollock stopped the video, found the correct frame and zoomed in on the two with the trunk. But their hoods were up, their heads were down, and it was impossible to see their faces. They looked like a couple of guys who had entered the floor amidst the earlier traffic. But that was of no help.

"Damn it! I'm in that trunk. I fucking know it," shouted Sharkey.

They decided that they'd seen enough. Pollock took the thumb drive with the girl's image, and said:

"Don't go away. I'll be back in 30 minutes."

Forty-five minutes passed before Pollock returned with a smile on his face:

"Got her! Her name is Clemencia and I know where she lives."

He handed a slip of paper to Sharkey with Clemencia's name and address, saying: "This is as far as I can go with you. You're on your own now. Be careful. If she's connected to people here who live by their own laws, I'd advise you to stay well clear of them."

"You'll need this to get access from security."

He gave Sharkey a plastic card, an approved access card that would gain them entry to the apartment complex where Clemencia lived.

Sharkey thanked Pollock, and stuck it in his pocket. Bill King got up and gave Pollock a hug. Then they left.

Thirty-five

Sharkey and King's expectations of Clemencia's address were far outmatched by the modern apartment complex that greeted them: a central swimming pool fronted the two story apartment building, each apartment with its own balcony; some overlooked the pool, others overlooked a winding path bordered by green lawn and flower beds. A pastoral setting only fifteen minutes from the Vegas Strip.

They showed their access card to the man sitting in the guard-house at the main gate and were waved through with no ceremony.

They reached the apartment number on Pollock's slip of paper and, without hesitation, King rang the door-bell. Sharkey stood to one side, out of view of the doorway. They expected that there would be a video view of the person standing in front of the door. Bill King did not appear threatening. That must have been the judgment inside the apartment because the door opened and a young lady stood there, inquisitively.

"Clemencia?" asked Bill.

"Yes?"

"I need to talk with you. May I come in?"

"No!" she said firmly and began to close the door.

At that moment Jim Sharkey stepped into view. Surprised, shocked, her face contorted, she tried to slam the door shut.

Too late. King pushed hard against her and forced his way inside, followed by Sharkey. Clemencia turned, ran back into the living room, and picked up a cell phone. But King grabbed her, knocked the phone out of her hand and forced her to sit down on the living room couch. She looked terrified and began to sob. Sharkey sat down, facing her.

"You remember me, don't you?"

She didn't answer, continued to sob.

"You drugged me in Caesar's. You do remember, don't you?"

She stared at him, her eyes large and fixated.

"And then you dumped me out in the Mojave. Left me there to die."

She groaned now, mumbling "no,no,no!"

"You planned to kill me, didn't you?"

She stopped sobbing, sat straight up, looked at him directly, and shouted:

"No! No! No!"

"But you drugged me. Who paid you to do that?"

Fear had now taken over. Sharkey could see the transformation. She'd stopped sobbing. But her lower lip trembled and her hands shook. She clasped them tightly, trying to suppress the shaking. Compelled by her fear, she started to talk:

"I didn't know anything. He told me that it was a joke. That you were a friend. And that drugging you was a practical joke. Please, please, I believed that. "

"What happened after you drugged me?"

"I don't know. I left the room then. That's what I was told to do."

"Who told you, Clemencia? Who paid you to do this? I need a name."

Clemencia stopped talking again. She sat mute. Silenced by fear,

"Do you want me to turn you over to the police?"

Struggling with herself, she blurted out, "But he'll kill me."

"No he won't. Because I'll kill him first."

Sharkey said that with such conviction that he could sense that she believed him. He continued:

"He intended to kill me. I accept that you didn't know that. But I need his name. You have a choice. I'll turn you over to the police or give me his name and I'll leave you alone."

"But he'll kill me."

"If I turn you over to the police he'll know about it and he'll kill you to keep your mouth shut. I need his name."

Sharkey took a deep breath and relaxed. King stood at the front window, looking out at the flowerbeds and the lawn, thinking that he could be anywhere but Las Vegas. Sharkey knew that Clemencia needed space to make a decision.

"Bruce Morgan."

"And where do I find this Bruce Morgan?"

"I don't know. I have no address. Or phone number."

"Come on, that's impossible. You get paid to drug me by a guy who doesn't exist."

"No, everybody knows Bruce Morgan."

"OK, what does he look like?"

But Clemencia said no more. It was as though she'd suddenly lost the ability to speak. She buried her head in her hands as her whole body started to tremble.

Sharkey realized that he'd come to the end. He had seen the fear in her eyes. But he was still angry. Angry enough to throttle her for drugging him. But he knew he'd have to walk away. So he left her with a threat: *told her that he wanted to strangle her for what she did and if she was hiding something, not telling him the truth, that he'd be back and she'd regret that ...*

Thirty-six

Bruce Morgan detested wimps and spineless women. Clemencia crying on his phone only added more ice to his already frozen heart.

"Stop it!"

He only had to say it once and the sobbing stopped.

"I don't have all day. What do you want?"

"That man …"

Morgan waited but he wouldn't wait long. Clemencia knew that. She pulled herself together. When she started to speak, it flowed from her.

"That man I drugged. Sharkey? The one you said you were playing a joke on."

"What about him?"

"He's here."

She paused but Morgan did not react. Total silence from him so she continued.

"He came to see me. Said I'd tried to kill him. I said it was a joke. He threatened me. Said he'd been dumped out in the Mojave and left to die."

Finally Morgan spoke.

"What did you say to him?"

"He was going to turn me in if I didn't tell him who paid me to drug him. I was afraid. I thought he might kill me."

"And you told him."

"I'm so sorry. Please forgive me. I have nowhere to turn now."

"Now he's looking for me."

"There's two of them. He has another guy with him. Never saw him before."

"You're fucking stupid! Do you hear me? You stay there. I'll come get you."

He hung up the phone.

Bruce Morgan did not take failure well. This was a big fail. Sharkey should have been picked clean by vultures by this time. He was angry at the two guys he'd paid – and paid well – to do the job. And he'd been paid very well by a good old buddy to take care of Sharkey. He'd have to clean this mess up. He picked up his phone and dialed:

"Joey, get Chet – and get your asses over here now!"

Twenty minutes later, they stood, looking nervous, very nervous, in front of him. Tough, muscle-bound, weight-lifters, they still seemed vulnerable. Joey was the talker, Chet the silent one. Joey stood, almost in a parade-rest stance, with his hands clasped behind his back. Chet slouched, head down, hands in pockets. They waited. Morgan gulped down the rest of his beer, set the empty bottle on the coffee table, and stood up.

"You fucked up the last job I gave you!"

Joey brought his hands to his side and almost gathered himself to attention. Chet shuffled from one foot to the other, trying to make his head disappear into the hoodie he wore. Neither of them spoke.

"The guy you dumped in the Mojave. He's back from the dead."

Joey refused to believe it, protesting "Can't be. We left him there, with nothing. Miles from anywhere. No water, no food, nothing. He couldn't have survived. He couldn't!"

"Well, he fucking did! A simple job. And you screwed up. He's here. Has a buddy with him. Clemencia couldn't keep her mouth shut. Now he's looking for me."

"Aw, shit," said Chet, the one who never spoke.

Morgan left them standing there, got another beer, took a swig out of it and said, "We're gonna tie up this loose end. And seal lips. I want this shut down."

Thirty-seven

The twins sat in their car on a very up-market street in a new development, out in the desert, only minutes from the Vegas Strip.

"Said he couldn't be found. That's what everybody said,"

Harvey was, as usual, reveling in the stupidity of people. He thought that all people were dumber than Hubert and himself.

"Money smartly spread around always opens mouths," said Hubert.

They had been waiting in their car, across the street from Bruce Morgan's house, for at least thirty minutes. They had been about to cross the street and enter the house when a car drove up, fast, and screeched to a halt in front of Morgan's house. Two muscle-bound types bounced out of the car and entered the house.

So they waited.

"Been in there for a while. What's going down?" A rhetorical question that Harvey did not expect to be answered.

So they waited.

They relaxed. They were prepared to wait. They reckoned that Morgan had a problem and surmised that Morgan's problem might just be their opportunity. Morgan's garage door swung out and up and a gleaming dark-blue Audi pulled out. It stopped momentarily. Enough time for them to see that there were three people in the car. Looked like the new arrivals in the back. They assumed that it was Morgan at the wheel. The Audi swung out on to the street and left. The twins followed.

Thirty-eight

Back in Vegas Sharkey and King contemplated their next move. It seemed simple: call Pollock. Bill reached him on his cell phone:

"Dave, do you know a Bruce Morgan?"

"Hah, everybody knows Bruce Morgan."

"Where can we find him?"

"Just hang out at Caesars – or anywhere on the Strip. He'll show up."

"No, we want to go to his home, where he lives."

"Agh, he lives anywhere, everywhere."

"What do you mean?"

"He doesn't have a fixed abode. Likes to keep on the move. He's not a vagrant. Not by a long shot. He's got millions, maybe billions. He's into everything: loan sharking, drugs, prostitution, real estate development, hedge funds. You name it. Legal and illegal. The Law knows it but they haven't been able to lay a finger on him. I'm sure he has some of them on his payroll. He's one clever son-of-a-bitch. But he's made enemies and some of them would like to kill him. That's another reason he seldom stays too long in one place. And the Pilkenroth twins want him too. When they asked me who to contact to find out if this Miller had run into trouble, owed the mob, that kind of thing. Only one guy. Morgan. I told them that."

"Talk to Jimmy."

He hands his phone to Sharkey who fills him in on their visit to Clemencia and how she had admitted that Morgan was the one who paid her to drug him. Claimed that she was told that the drugging was a prank on a good friend. Sharkey remained skeptical and highly doubted that Clemencia really believed that.

"Look Dave, I believe that this Bruce Morgan dumped me in the Mojave. To die. Those two thugs you saw on the video. I'll bet they worked for him. And, as I said, when I saw it, I'm sure I was in that damn case they were trundling into the elevator."

"OK, let's say you're right. And you do find Morgan. Do you realize that you'll be committing suicide if you make a move against him?"

"I'll run with that risk. I need to know if Miller sent him to get rid of me. I need to know that. Now where do I find him?"

"I don't know. But I think Clemencia knows more than she told you. I'll bet she knows where he is. And maybe she's off now to warn him."

"So you think she lied to me."

"It's possible."

"Maybe I should pay her another visit."

"The twins are after him too. I just told Bill about it. He'll fill you in. Believe me, you do not want to get caught between Morgan and the twins. The odds would be stacked against you."

Despite Pollock's warnings, Sharkey was committed. And Bill King would stand with him. They both knew that. They turned around and headed back toward Clemencia's.

"So who are these twins?" King voiced what they were both wondering.

"Gotta be working for the H-R company. And that means that H-R already knows about its missing millions. They told a cock and bull story to Pollock. MetroBank must have discovered that I broke into their funds transfer system. But how did they find out about Miller. There was no trail between him and me."

"And what's this Roger Coleman stuff?"

"Never heard the name before. But it wouldn't surprise me to find out that Miller was not his name. I never questioned how he came by his inside knowledge of H-R. I didn't care. I'd reached such a shit place in my life that I did not care. Do you understand that Bill? I did not care."

"That's what I find so hard to believe. The Sparks I knew in the Gulf would never have fallen into a dark place like that. But you're out of it now."

"I'll never let the bastards grind me down again. "

"But where is Miller? Or who is Miller?"

"Remember I called a good friend in Boston before we left your home. His name is Owen MacDara and he has strong connections in Washington. I asked him to find out about Miller. I reckoned that Miller pulled a con, that he knew too much about H-R, and that probably Miller wasn't his name. Being dumped in the Mojave brought me back to my senses. I needed to get Miller. Reckoned that Vegas was a good place to start but, just in case I hit a dead end here, I figured that Owen might be able to locate the bastard. And I wanted Owen to look in on Sally and the kids as well."

"So have you heard from him yet?"

"I told him not to try and contact me, said I'd call him instead. I'll give him a few more days."

Halfway to Clemencia's King abruptly pulled off the road into a parking lot beside a roadside motel. Sharkey's face frowned into a question.

"Sharks, I figure that we better be prepared. Don't know who might be waiting for us at Clemencia's."

He got out, opened the trunk, picked up the small sports bag and returned to the driver's seat. Settled in, he opened the sports bag and handed one of the Beretta M9s to Sharkey. He handed him another fifteen round magazine.

"You think we need to be carrying."

"I do. I think this Morgan character might attempt to finish the job."

Sharkey knew that King was right. He hadn't handled the M9 since the Gulf but it sat snug in his hand. Comfortable. Like an old glove that he'd just re-discovered. He slipped the extra magazine into his pocket. King pulled the car out of the parking lot and they headed for Clemencia's.

Thirty-nine

Clemencia was unhappy with the way her call to Bruce Morgan had ended. She sunk into a heap, her mind frozen as though someone had hit a pause button in her head.

But some lingering spark restarted the fire inside her. She had only two options: stay or flee. If she felt safe, she'd stay. But she did not feel safe. She was afraid. Afraid of Bruce Morgan's vengeance. She'd seen it before. She knew she had to flee. Forty-five minutes had passed while her mind had been frozen. Time was against her. She ran into her bedroom, dumped a suitcase onto the bed, and opened it. Frantically, she grabbed clothes and other essentials and dumped them into the case. She already had the most important things in her shoulder bag: passport, check-book, credit cards, cash.

She looked around, longingly, at all those pictures, knick-knacks, and personal things that make a place a home. She couldn't take any of that with her.

As Clemencia was preparing to leave Bruce Morgan's car ground to a fast stop outside. Morgan jumped out of the car, followed by Joey and Chet. Clemencia emerged, pulling her suitcase behind her. Too late, she saw them running towards her.

"Going somewhere!"

Morgan's voice had a sneering quality.

She froze again. Stopped dead. Nowhere to run. In her heart, she knew. Knew that it was all over.

Morgan grasped her arm and took her door keys. Chet pulled her suitcase. Joey followed.

All of this unfolded as the twins watched from their car across the street. They had followed Bruce Morgan and his two thugs.

"Some shit's about to go down," said Harvey, whose language reverted to street level at times like this. Almost a preparation, like adrenalin, to prepare him for the fight ahead.

"Guess we'd better intervene." Hubert, a man of few words, stated the facts calmly. He reached behind him and picked up their weapons: the Walther P-38 for himself and the Browning P-35 High Power for Harvey. They wore flexible nitrile rubber gloves to hide their fingerprints.

Clemencia slumped into her couch in the living room. Morgan continued to berate her. She didn't answer. Her eyes were dead. She didn't cry. She didn't whimper. She didn't move a finger.

"I trusted you. And you know I don't trust very many people. But you sold me out. Now this Sharkey, and whoever else he's in league with, will be after me. I don't like having to look over my shoulder. I make other people look over theirs. Many have tried to bring me down. They all failed. But now, a little whore like you may have succeeded where others failed."

He stopped his tirade and looked at Chet. One nod of his head meant that he expected them to tidy up this mess. Chet crossed the floor and moved behind Clemencia. Hand over her mouth, he lifted her up from the couch.

He held her there, suspended in slow motion, as the door crashed open and the twins entered firing. Clemencia slid out of his arms as he dived behind the couch, taking his own gun from his shoulder holster. Screaming, "Joey, Joey," Chet opened fire. Too late. Joey was already sprawled on the floor, blood forming a pool under his head. The twins had taken cover and were shooting at him from both sides of the room.

In the chaos, Morgan ran out of the room.

Hubert followed, leaving Harvey to deal with Chet.

Morgan ran onto Clemencia's balcony and looked down at the drop to the ground below. No hard ground. Only soft clay where the bed of flowers bloomed. He decided to jump.

Hubert caught up with him before he jumped.

Morgan stared at the gun.

Hubert held it firmly with both hands, pointing it directly at him.

He couldn't miss.

But Morgan had been in many tight corners and always maneuvered his way out of them. He'd never seen this man before and he wondered who had sent him. He had enemies. But they'd never tried a hit on him like this before. In broad daylight too. He reckoned that they didn't want him dead. If they had, this guy would have pulled the trigger already. That gave him a choice.

"Who are you? What do you want?"

"Who I am doesn't matter, Bruce Morgan."

"What do you want?"

"Answers. We want answers. We need to find a person that we believe you know."

"And you're threatening my life because of that?"

"No, we would prefer to be civilized. But we thought we should stop you and your thugs from trying to kill that young lady. I'm sure she might have answered our questions."

"Young lady! My ass! Put that gun down and get the fuck out of here."

Hubert lowered the gun. Maybe Morgan would talk if he used the civilized approach. Morgan knew he had a choice. The shooting had stopped and he hoped that Chet had taken care of this guy's partner. He slid his hand behind his back and unsheathed a knife. Superbly fit, with a black belt in karate, he felt that he had the advantage.

Hubert was unprepared.

Morgan took a classic karate stance and, knife in right hand, kicked straight out with his left foot, knocking the gun from Hubert's hand.

Hubert jumped away, barely escaping the slash of the knife. Knowing that he was no match for Morgan, he dived across the floor and tried to reach his gun. But Morgan kicked him hard in the ribs and he doubled over in pain.

Suddenly he felt Morgan crash to the floor beside him and saw the knife slither across the floor. Shocked, he looked up to see Harvey standing over him, holding a brass candle in his hand.

Morgan was out cold.

Hubert winced in pain as Harvey helped him to his feet. They tied Morgan's hands behind his back with zip ties. Secure and inescapable. They'd take him somewhere and ask him questions that they were sure he wouldn't refuse to answer. He remained unconscious as they carried him through the living room. Everyone was dead. Chet and Joey in pools of their own blood. Clemencia had died first, struck by a bullet from someone's gun. If it hadn't been the bullet that took her life, then it would have been at the hands of Chet. She was destined to die today. They stood Morgan upright, held him close between them and walked him to their car. They found his house keys and car keys in his pocket. Decided to leave his car and take him home.

Minutes after they left the street, two cop cars flew in and screeched to a halt. Four cops bailed out and, guns at the ready, ran towards Clemencia's apartment.

Forty

Four distinctive black and white Ford Crown Victoria police cars dominated the road outside Clemencia's apartment as Sharkey and King drove up. Unable to pass, they halted a sensible distance away and watched the scene. They didn't need to say anything. They knew. Morgan, or somebody, had gotten to Clemencia. But they didn't know the extent of the carnage. They couldn't get in to her apartment and it was unwise to ask the cops what was going on. Sharkey needed to stay under the radar.

So they waited and watched. White coated officers entered and exited, carrying a variety of objects. The pathologist and forensic folks soon arrived in two more vehicles.

"Can't be all this attention for Clemencia," King said.

"Naw, somethin' big went down in there."

"This guy Morgan. Couldn't be him, could it?"

"A shrewd power broker like him. Doubt it."

"Yeah, but I'll bet Clemencia called him after we left."

"I reckon."

"Bet he knows you're still alive."

"You think he'll try to finish the job."

"Well, I wouldn't want a loose cannon like you running around."

"Then he probably sent his thugs to talk to Clemencia."

"OK. But what happened in there?"

That was a rhetorical question. They decided that they'd better get out of there. They turned their car, quietly, and headed back to the Strip. Back to Caesars.

Forty-one

Hubert and Harvey stood inside Bruce Morgan's wine bar looking at the rows of red and white. Exuberant, Harvey said:

"Must be three hundred bottles, at least."

"Ah, but look at the labels."

They chose the Chateau Lafite Rothschild. Two bottles. Decided to have one each. They selected two Waterford Crystal glasses. Only the best would do. Harvey uncorked both bottles, swearing that his rubber gloves felt like condoms.

They finished their first glass in silence. Pouring their second glass, Hubert said:

"Guess they'd planned to silence her."

"That's a good bet."

"She's dead now anyway."

"Collateral damage."

"Damn shame. I hate collateral damage. No satisfaction in it at all."

"Guess she knew where the bodies are."

"You mean Miller and Sharkey."

"I don't give a shit about Sharkey. It's Miller we want, or Coleman, or whatever his name is."

Groans interrupted them.

"Our guest is awake."

"Yeah, time to have a chat."

They walked back to the utility room and opened the door. Morgan was still tied to the chair. He'd pushed it back against the washing machine and dryer, trying to find a sharp edge to use on his cuffs. His face, red and blotched, added to the ferocious glare in his eyes.

"You bastards! You'll pay for this! That's a promise!"

Harvey laughed out loud, saying:

"You're in no position to issue warnings, dear Brucie."

"Do you know who I am? Do you know who you're fucking with?"

"Brucie, we know all about you. And we don't care if you're the King of Siam."

"Then you're fucking stupid. You're signing your own death warrant ."

At that promise, both twins started to laugh uncontrollably. Morgan's eyes were popping out of his head. The bastards were laughing at him. He tried to speak but his tongue failed him and foamy saliva slid out of the corners of his mouth.

Finally the twins stopped laughing and stared at Bruce Morgan. Hubert spoke this time:

"You cannot make demands. We'd have expected you to realize that by this time. Nobody knows you're missing. And nobody is coming to rescue you."

Harvey grabbed a towel from the rack in the utility room and wiped the saliva from Morgan's mouth. Then they waited.

Morgan spat out the words, "What do you want from me?"

Harvey looked at Hubert and said, "Show him the photos."

Hubert took out two photos, the one taken by the security camera and a better one of Coleman, emailed to them from Carlos. He held the photos in front of Morgan's eyes. Morgan hid his surprise. He was looking at the face of his friend Tommy Gordon-Smith.

"Where is he?"

"I don't know him," spluttered Morgan.

"He was travelling with another man called Sharkey. Sharkey checked into Caesars about ten days ago. For one night only. What do you know about him?"

Morgan had gained his courage again. There was no way he was going to rat on his friend, Tommy. That's one thing you never do. Rat on a friend. If that's all these mad twins wanted, he'd stall them. He was certain that his people would get him. And get him soon.

He sat up straight in the chair and said, "I don't know what the fuck you're talking about. I don't know this man. Never saw him before. And I know nothing about any Shark, or whatever you call him."

Harvey looked at Hubert and sadly shook his head. Their body language expressed defeat. Enough to fool Morgan into thinking that they'd let him go. But he'd soon find out that he was badly mistaken.

Forty-two

Dave Pollock came to Sharkey and King's room as soon as they called him. They described the scene at Clemencia's. He called his contact in the police and got the details. They could see his face change, darken almost, as he listened. Finished, he turned with a great sigh and said:

"You're lucky you weren't there."

"What happened?"

"Carnage! Three dead. Clemencia and two thugs. From their description, looks like they're the guys who dumped you in the Mojave."

"And Morgan?"

"No sign of him. Don't even know if he'd been there."

"But who did this?"

"The police don't know. They're interviewing neighbors. But there are very few around at this time of day."

"No shit! So it's a mystery."

"Not in my books. My bet's on the twins."

At that thought, Pollock shut up. King and Sharkey looked at each other, knowing that they were on the same wavelength. Sharkey expressed their thoughts:

"These twins are a tough act. What's your bet that they've got Morgan."

Pollock looked surprised. It was obvious that he hadn't considered that.

"Damn it. You could be right."

"If we are, my bet's on the twins."

"And Morgan knows who this Miller guy is ..."

"That's why we think they've got him."

They all reflected on that, until Pollock said:

"That could be either good or bad for you, Jimmy."

"You think."

"Sure. If they take Morgan out of the game, then he won't be after you."

"And if Morgan talks."

"That's good too. If he talks, he'll give them Miller. That's what they really want."

"And if he doesn't talk."

"Then I'm afraid the twins will come after you. That's the bad."

Forty-three

The large bathtub stood alone on intricately carved legs. They had rigged a strap around it, just as you would a large suitcase. Rigged to strap him into the tub. Yet strong enough to support Morgan's weight and stable enough to hold him, feet up, head down. A huge pillow helped to elevate him. *A dry run*, they thought. Give him an introduction. Teach him the wisdom of talking to them.

Hubert picked up a soft wet cloth and draped it over his face. Harvey held him tightly as Hubert held a large water jug, ready to pour.

"Bruce, we don't want to do this. Tell us the name. That's all."

Nothing.

"Kick your feet when you've had enough."

Hubert started to pour the water slowly over Morgan's face. He reckoned that Morgan wouldn't last long.

But he was wrong. Morgan refused to kick his feet. He strained against the strap that held him. Fists clenched and face distorted, he tried to close his throat and repel the water. They did not intend to kill him so they stopped. Releasing the strap, they pulled him out of the tub and dumped him on the floor.

On his knees, Bruce Morgan coughed and coughed. And vomited everything in his stomach.

Forty-four

Sharkey decided it was time to call Owen MacDara. Maybe Owen had some answers. He assumed that Owen was still with Sally. That didn't bother him. It had been over for a long time between Sally and himself. In his heart he thought that maybe he'd get to talk to his kids. That's if they wanted to talk to him. Owen answered the phone on the second ring.

"Owen, Jimmy."

"About time you called. I was about to send out a posse. Where are you?"

"Vegas. It's a long story. Did you find out anything?"

"I found out who Miller really is."

Sharkey let that sink in before he said anything. He could hear Owen breathing on the other end, holding the answer like a prize. Well, he thought, Owen is entitled to covet this. Must have used all his connections.

"I can wait."

"It's complicated. Miller is Roger Coleman. The same guy who was thrown out of H-R. He was about to wed Elena Himmler-Ramos. But the brothers, Carlos and Eduardo, found out that he was a fraud and a con-man."

"When you say 'thrown out' …"

"My sources tell me that Carlos and Eduardo escorted him from H-R and put him on a flight back to England. Told him not to show his face again for the good of his health."

"But he didn't leave the country."

"Yeah. You know that. Must have given them the slip. Showed up as Miller and trapped you into diverting those H-R millions. Truly an act of revenge. And he didn't give a shit about you, Jimmy. You reached a new low on this one. What were you thinking?"

"I wasn't thinking. I had hit rock bottom, the lowest point of my life. I just did not give a good fuck!"

Jimmy's voice thickened at this admission and his eyes turned bleary. Owen could sense it. So he gave Jimmy time to compose himself.

"Jimmy, you learned a hard lesson. You'll never sink that low again. I know you, bro. And I have faith."

Jimmy did not know how to answer that. But he got a grip on himself, wiped his eyes, and said:

"Owen, you're the best."

No need to answer that one. So Owen picked up where he had left off.

"Roger Coleman did not go to Vegas. He took a flight to London the same day that he told you he'd gone to Vegas."

"Went back home. Hah."

"In a way. But the real Roger Coleman never left England."

Jimmy could sense that Owen was enjoying the revelations. He could feel it in his voice.

"So who the fuck is he?"

"Ah, ha…my sources uncovered that too. His real name is Tom Gordon-Smith. He's a con-man, a thief, a gambler. He checked into the Cadogan Hotel in Knightsbridge the day he arrived. Only stayed a few days. Checked out and disappeared."

"So you don't know where he is."

"That's right. We don't know."

"But he must have a back-story. Tell me whatever you know about him."

"Seems he's a chip off the old block. His father owns a chain of bookie shops in England. He was also a champion poker player. Used to fly regularly to Vegas to compete."

"Ah..."

"Yeah, you're right. He'd take young Tommy with him. Tommy spent a lot of time in Vegas. Played some poker too. Hung out with all the wrong people. Knows the place well."

"So that's why he picked Vegas. He had a local gambler and crook called Bruce Morgan take care of me. Must have paid him well to dispose of me."

"Sure. He conned you. And took the money for himself."

"H-R found out about him, and me too. They're out to get him."

"My advice to you, Jimmy, is this – stay out of it. MetroBank did not report their missing money to the local cops or the Feds. Neither they nor H-R want any publicity. That's good. The Law is not looking for you, Jimmy."

Jimmy did not reply to that. He had anticipated what Owen would say. He'd already made up his mind. And he would not let Owen dissuade him.

"How's Sally, Sarah and Ronan?"

"They're OK. But they're worried as hell. They didn't know what happened to you. Little Ronan misses you most, I think."

"I know that. I do. Sally got over me a long time ago. But I sure miss the kids. Try to explain to them. Tell them that I'm OK, that I'm safe and well. Tell them that I have to go on a foreign trip for a while. But tell them I'll be back soon again. Take care of Sally. And give Ronan a hug from me. Will you do that, Owen?"

"Dammit, Jimmy! I knew you wouldn't take my advice."

"I'm in your debt on this one, Owen. Don't even know how I'll repay you."

Neither of them knew how to end the phone call. So they waited, silently. Finally, Owen said: "Look, Jimmy, if you insist on following that bastard to England, I'll keep digging over there."

"Thanks, Owen."

With that they ended the call.

Forty-five

Hubert pressed Morgan's chest, harder and harder, trying to force the water out of his lungs. It was futile. He had no pulse. He was gone.

They decided to make it look like an accident in the bath, even though they knew that an autopsy would probably prove otherwise. The cleaned out the bathtub and filled it with warm soapy water. Then they removed all of Morgan's clothes and slid him into the water, letting his head submerge

They removed all evidence of the waterboarding. Back in the utility room, they emptied Morgan's pockets and put his clothes in the washing machine.

In the kitchen, they put the empty wine bottles and the two glasses in a black plastic garbage bag, tied it and took it with them. Leave no trace behind. That's the dictum they lived by.

In their car, Harvey looked at Hubert and said:

"He wasn't as tough as he thought."

"Right. But we didn't intend to kill him."

"Better this way. Shut his mouth for good."

"At least he coughed up the name we wanted."

"In his last breath!"

They considered that. Then they both started to laugh. It tickled their macabre humor.

"Tommy Gordon-Smith. Good English sounding name."

They disposed of the black garbage bag in the dumpster farthest away from Morgan's. At their hotel, they packed, filed a flight plan to Teterboro Airport, and called Carlos.

"I still think of him as Coleman. Where is he?"

"He never made it to Vegas."

"So what's Vegas all about?"

"As far as we can figure it out, he sent Sharkey to Vegas. Said he'd meet him here. But he paid Morgan to get rid of Sharkey. You'll find his bones somewhere in the Mojave."

"Good job! That's all we can do on this end. Our European operations will take over. Your usual fee will be remitted to your account today."

"Thank you Carlos. It was a fun gig!"

Carlos said no more, simply thought in his own head '*insane fuckers, but they do provide a vital service.*'

Two hours later Hubert and Harvey climbed out of the clouds in northern Nevada, put their plane on autopilot and sat back in satisfaction at a job well done.

Forty-six

Now that Sharkey was sure that the feds were not looking for him, he felt safe enough to use his ATM card. He had seventy-five grand linked to his New York checking account, sufficient funds to last him for a while. Next he made a reservation at the Cadogan Hotel and booked a flight to London.

Bags packed, he met Bill King at the bar for a final beer or two. Hoisting their first and clinking glasses, Bill said,

"Sure'd like to be goin' with you, Sharks."

"I know you can't, but thanks for the thought."

"I'd like to stop you. These H-R bastards are dangerous."

"I don't plan to go up against them. I just want to get to Miller before they do. Then I don't give a shit what they do to him. That's if there's anything left after I get done with him."

Sharkey knew it was bravado. And he knew that King too knew it was bravado. But they both knew it was the kind of bravado that all men used when embarking on dangerous missions. Like going to war. And Sharkey knew he was going to war.

So they talked about old times, shared memories, and battles fought and won. Towards the end, they had gotten sentimental and Sharkey could find no adequate way to thank Bill King for all he had done.

Notified that his taxi waited, he clutched Bill in a tight hug, picked up his bag, and walked towards the door as Bill shouted after him, "Call me when you get back!"

Forty-seven

Tears turned Sharkey's eyes moist as the London taxi circled Sloane Square and turned right towards the Cadogan Hotel. Seventeen years ago. He remembered. He and Sally had decided on Europe for their honeymoon. Dublin, London, Paris. Three magical weeks. That memory dried the tears and brought laughter lines to the corner of his eyes.

As he climbed out of the taxi at the Cadogan Hotel, it all felt so familiar. The ambiance had not changed in seventeen years. The courtesy. The gentle civility. So different from the brash, in-your-face America. But he knew that, despite the difference, he loved both cultures.

He was jetlagged but he had no time to indulge that. So he decided to brave it out for the day. With little to unpack, he was back at the reception desk in twenty minutes. The young Assistant Manager raised his eyebrows,

"Is there anything we can do for you, sir?"

"Yes, I hope you can. A good friend stayed here last week and I'd love to get in touch with him. I don't have his London number and, unfortunately, I don't have his address either."

Taken aback by the request, the young man looked at Sharkey, in an attempt to make a judgment. Deciding that Sharkey seemed trustworthy, he said,

"We're not permitted to disclose private information. But, if you can describe your friend to me, I will see if there is any public information available that I can share with you."

"His name is Tom Gordon-Smith. Probably stayed one or two nights."

Sharkey waited while the young Assistant Manager checked the register and other hotel documents. Finally, he turned back to face Sharkey and said,

"Yes, your friend did stay here. Two nights. He received only one phone call. From the United States, Las Vegas. He left no forwarding address or telephone information. Sorry, I can't be more helpful."

Jimmy thanked him. For nothing. Or maybe not. The phone call from Vegas was new information. He wondered what that might have been. A progress update from Bruce Morgan. *Could I be right,* he thought. *Could it be that simple? If I'm right, my Miller man now believes that I am rotting somewhere in the Mojave desert! And, that means that H-R will think the same. Which gives me a great advantage. I am the man who doesn't exist!*

With no information to work on, Jimmy decided that he should conserve his energy, eke out the day, absorb a little of London life. He walked out of the hotel into a dull, dry afternoon. Perfect for a stroll. In a few minutes he was in Sloane Square, the gateway to the alternative, lifestyle of Chelsea. He walked around the square, clockwise, until he reached The Royal Court Theatre. The memories flooded back again. Sally and he had been to a literary evening, mostly poetry readings, in the main theatre. Having enjoyed it so much they went to a play two nights later. In the upper 'theatre in the round' space where the audience and the actors shared the same space, making one feel as though they were part of the ensemble.

Jolted out of his reverie by a dislodgement of people from the nearby underground tube station, and assaulted by a newsagent shouting out the day's incendiary headlines from the local tabloids, Sharkey moved on. He completed his circle of the square and walked on the King's Road into Chelsea. Replete with cool, funky boutiques and cool, funky people, he indulged all his senses. International cuisine invaded his nostrils from a variety of small bistros and cafes. Fuelling his appetite, he settled for Italian, the cuisine he liked best. A mouth-watering lasagna, a small green salad, some good red wine, and he was satisfied. The small table at the window let him relish the passers-by as he savored the last of his wine.

By the time he got back to the Cadogan Hotel, he felt a sense of serenity. Tommy Gordon-Smith had disappeared from his memory. Then he noticed the red light flashing on his phone, announcing that he had had a phone call. He rang the front desk and was informed that a Mr Owen MacDara had called from the United States.

He returned the call and Owen answered immediately.

"Did I wake you?" he said, humor in his voice.

"Wake me? You're bad. Just got back here. Been down in Chelsea, soaking up London again."

"Got news for you. My sources don't know where Gordon-Smith may be. Best bet is to start with Gordon-Smith Sr. His old man owns a niche group of bookmaker joints. Six in all. Not your average walk-in betting shops. They're furnished in a very eclectic fashion. His first, his flagship joint, G-S Bookmakers, is in Camden Town. Camden is a vibrant place, Great food and drink. They tell me that G-S Senior hangs out in Joyce's Pub. It's the only one that has stayed traditional, no music gigs, no sports blaring at you from the TV. And it's next door to G-S Bookmakers."

"Nobody here could help me. They confirmed that he'd stayed here. And that he'd received a call from the States. From Vegas."

MacDara let out a whistle of surprise.

"Are you thinking what I am?"

"Bruce Morgan?"

"Absolutely."

"Giving his friend Tommy an update"

"Yeah! Offering condolences on my demise."

"A little perverse."

"What do you mean?"

"Bruce Morgan is dead. Drowned in his bathtub. Or made to look like that."

"The twins! They killed him, didn't they?"

"That would be my bet. But they'll never prove it. Whoever did it applied the best cleaner job to the place. They won't find a thing. Not even a hair."

"But Bruce must have talked. Given them Miller's real name."

"And, if the twins were working for the Himmler-Ramos gang, then H-R will soon be in England to get him. And they won't just settle for their money back. He's a dead man."

"I figure, if Bruce said nothing about me, they will assume that my bones are being picked by the vultures out in the Mojave."

"Maybe, just maybe. But you are in very dangerous territory, Jimmy. I told you to give this up."

"I can't. I just can't. The bastard tried to have me killed. I can't walk away."

"But he's a dead man walking,"

"And I want to look him in the eyes while he's still alive!"

MacDara simply sighed in resignation, then said:

"I have a house in London. Haven't used it in a long time. I bought it ten years ago. My company, GMA, had a lot of clients here and London was our European headquarters. I don't like living in hotels. It seemed just right, near the Royal Albert Hall, a stone's throw from Knightsbridge and Chelsea and five minutes from the West End. I didn't offer it to you when you told me you were going. I still hoped that you would give up. But now that you have decided to pursue this bastard, I want you to use my house as your base. It's on Alexandra Place, not far from your hotel. Mrs. Simpson looks after the place for me. I've told her to expect you."

Jimmy Sharkey said nothing for a minute. He had a lump in his throat, a little overwhelmed by Owen's support.

"Owen, you're too much. A beer or two in your local pub hardly seems adequate any more."

"A beer or two will be more than enough. And I want to make sure you get back to enjoy them. So there's an item at the house that I want you to have. It's in a wall safe behind my desk. Mrs. Simpson has an envelope for you with the combination."

Forty-eight

Next morning Jim Sharkey checked out of the Cadogan Hotel and walked to Owen's house. He rang the doorbell. Almost immediately the door opened and a petite, silver haired lady with an open, inviting face greeted him.

"You must be Mr. Sharkey?"

"Yes, Mrs. Simpson. Mr. MacDara said you'd expect me."

"Please do come in."

Owen lifted his case through the door and left it in the hall, as advised by Mrs. Simpson. She said she wanted to familiarize him with the house, make him feel at home. On the first floor, a stainless steel high-tech kitchen, balanced by butcher block counters, was separated from a library that also functioned as a living room, by a pine paneled walk-in wine bar that must have had at least two hundred bottles in a floor-to-ceiling rack. An open dining room adjoined the kitchen. The master bedroom, with its own Jacuzzi bathtub, dominated the second floor. A door led to a small attached office. Mrs. Simpson told Sharkey that he would be using the master bedroom.

The third floor was MacDara's own private art gallery, housing both paintings and sculptures. Some fine soapstone carvings sat on display stands at strategic points but it was the paintings that dominated, all abstract or post-modern.

Tour finished, Mrs. Simpson invited Sharkey to the kitchen for tea.

"Or perhaps you would prefer coffee?"

"No, Mrs. Simpson. Tea would be fine, thank you."

As she prepared the tea, she chatted away, "I'll leave you the front and back door keys and the instructions on the alarm system. Owen asked me to give you this envelope as well. The house is all yours. The cleaning lady arrives at 9am every Friday. Usually stays about two hours. I'll also leave you my home and mobile phone numbers in case you need to contact me. The kitchen is well stocked, refrigerator and freezer, so you shouldn't want for anything."

Leaving Jim with a pot of tea, a fine china cup and saucer, milk, sugar, and a selection of biscuits, she wished him well and left.

Jim Sharkey thought he was dreaming. Sipping the tea, his life in recent weeks flashed through his mind. His fall from grace at MetroBank, his entrapment by Miller, his near-death experience in the Mojave, the madness in Vegas, his cramped and often lonely little apartment in lower Manhattan, and now this luxury in the heart of London.

But the stark reality of the reason he had come to London soon banished the dreaming. He picked up the white envelope and headed for Owen's office, wondering what secret the wall safe contained.

The wall safe was embedded in the stone wall, behind one of many awards that adorned the wall behind Owen's desk. Using the combination, he unlocked the safe. A folded leather wrap, tied with lace-like leather sat inside. Sharkey took it out and opened it. The secret was no surprise. A Glock 17. He picked it up and felt the light polymer weapon in his hand. It felt comfortable, familiar. It had been his secondary weapon of choice in the Gulf. Even though it had not been standard equipment, the Army 'looked the other way'.

Four double-stack magazines, each holding 17 rounds, nestled at the back of the safe. And, last but not least, a shoulder holster with a double-mag pouch. He tried on the holster, inserted the Glock and a double-stack mag, and slipped on his jacket. Felt comfortable. Nothing obvious. Good to go!

Forty-nine

Zurich, Switzerland

Horst Richter, CEO of Himmler-Ramos International, sat in his office sipping his late-morning coffee as he perused the 'to be read' stack in his in-box. No meetings, no fires to put out. He seldom relaxed. Even now he felt idle. Still he knew that he used these infrequent quiet times for mental renewal. Just as he used his early morning three-mile runs. Swiveling his chair around to face the large tenth floor window behind him, he looked out over the river Limmat. The city spread out before him. Even though Berne was the capital, to him Zurich was the real capital; the financial heart, the pacemaker of Himmler-Ramos International. The buzzing intercom broke his contemplation. Turning back to his desk, he picked up his phone.

"Ja, Judith?"

"Carlos on the phone from Asuncion."

"Put him through to me, please."

He knew this was not going to be a social call so he decided to take it standing. Taking the phone in his hand, he stood up and looked out across the Limmat into the far distance.

"Are you sitting down?" Carlos was serious.

"No. If I anticipate what you are about to tell me, I want to be standing up." It was obvious to Carlos that Horst was equally serious.

"We know who stole our money. No stranger. He was a member of our H-R family. Worse than that, he was almost a member of our own family."

"Who is this traitor?"

"You knew him as Roger Coleman."

"That con-man! The one who was going to marry Elena?"

"*Bastardo!* He duped a MetroBank exec, a jerk called Sharkey. Used him to gain access to their security and encryption systems. Sent Sharkey to Vegas. Must have promised to split our money with him. But he never intended to give Sharkey a penny. Hired a Vegas gangster, friend of his, to take care of Sharkey. We believe Sharkey's bones are rotting somewhere in the Mojave desert."

"Did the twins uncover this?"

"Yes. They persuaded the Vegas gangster to answer their questions. He didn't survive the interrogation. That wasn't planned but we think it's for the best. The twins like to do a thorough clean-up after every operation. None of this will get back to us or our company."

"Where is Coleman now?"

"We believe he's in London. And Coleman is not his name. His real name is Tom Gordon-Smith. Morgan coughed that up before his departure."

"Where is our money?"

"We don't know. Cox was our man at Metro, as you know. He failed us. He was the first lead we got on Coleman. Photos of a disguised Coleman at a cash machine. That's all. No trace on the missing funds transfers."

"Why do we have an incompetent like that in our employ?"

"We don't anymore. Cox was an exposure that we could not afford. He knew too much. The twins took care of him for us."

"So we don't know how Coleman, or whatever his name is, moved our money. We don't know if it's still in North America. Or maybe right under our noses here in Switzerland."

"You're right. Only Gordon-Smith knows that. And he's now in your jurisdiction. I wish he wasn't. I would love to watch him die. Slowly."

"Oh, he will die. I told you in Paraguay that *we will have blood*."

"We're looking into Gordon-Smith's background. If he was friends with this Vegas gangster, there has to be a backstory there. But I'm sure you might have more success on his home ground in Europe."

"We will move on that immediately. We may have a serious impediment though. The assets I intended to deploy do not have the cross-border freedoms that we used to enjoy. This *al-Qaeda* madness has made us all prisoners. But you can help"

"What can I do?"

"The Pilkenroth twins. How would they like a trip to Europe?"

Carlos did not answer immediately. But it dawned on him that they were a brilliant asset. An asset that always stayed above the radar. An asset that always delivered. So he said what he was thinking.

"That's brilliant. They can cross borders with impunity."

"Good. Ask them to call me."

Horst Richter did not engage in small talk. Carlos knew that and did not even try. The phone call stayed brief, economical, and essential. As soon as Carlos hung up, Horst picked up the phone and dialled a number he had committed to memory.

"I need to see you."

"Now. It's important."

"I need *vital research* done immediately."

His contact knew what he wanted. *Vital research* were the key words.

Fifty

Camden Town, London.

It was a typical London afternoon when Jim Sharkey reached Camden. Scattered showers and intermittent sunshine. People of all ages, sexes, and colors crowded the streets, making an impressionist canvas for the eyes. Despite diversions and attractions everywhere, he stayed focused, and located *G-S Bookmakers* within ten minutes. Once inside he understood why it was called unique. A full size statue of a horse dominated the center, a counter built from church pews fronted the punters' seats, salvaged from old tractors. Various antiques from the racing world of times past adorned the walls.

An ornate, stained glass door, labelled ' staff private' sat in the wall adjacent to the counter. Sharkey knocked, then turned the handle. But it was locked.

The place was almost empty. Two elderly men stood staring at the twelve-screen SIS system, looking baffled.

Jim approached a young man behind the counter,

"Excuse me. I'm looking for Mr. Gordon-Smith."

The young man looked him up and down before he decided to answer him.

"You missed him. He's gone for the day. Won't be here again till tomorrow."

"Do you know when?"

"No, he didn't say."

Jim decided there was little point in continuing this conversation. It was a dead-end. He walked out and stood for a minute. The sign for *Joyce's Pub*, enshrined in an Irish harp, hung prominently a few doors away. *Why not*, he thought, *I might get lucky.*

What a contrast, he thought, as soon as he opened the door. Wall to wall people, talking, laughing, drinking. He sidled his way up to the bar and squeezed his way between two people who didn't seem to object. Catching the very busy bartender's eye, he waited.

"Yes, what can I get you?"

"A pint of Guinness …and I'd also like to speak to Tom Gordon-Smith. Is he here?"

"Over in that corner. If you can fight your way."

He waited as his Guinness was slowly poured forming a perfect head. Savoring a sip, he maneuvered his way towards a large round table at the far corner of the pub. A large well-fed man seemed to be holding court with four others. Talking expansively, there could be no mistake. Bald with white tufts of hair where sideburns should be, his bushy black eyebrows almost presented a comical image, were it not for the eyes. Cold and penetrating, they did not smile even when the rest of his face was doing so. He had found Tom Gordon-Smith. He moved close to the table, stood at the side, and waited for an opportune moment.

"Mr. Gordon-Smith, can I speak to you privately?"

"Do I know you?"

"No, you don't."

"Do you owe me money?"

"No."

"Do I owe you money."

"No."

"Good. In my business, it's always best to get these things settled. Now we can talk."

"I'd prefer to speak to you privately."

"This is my office. These are my friends. What is this about?"

"It's about Tom, your son."

A dead silence descended over the table. The other three men shuffled uncomfortably. One got up and said, "Think we should leave you for a while."

Then all four left the table and Sharkey took a seat facing Tom Gordon-Smith who had sat silent since hearing his son's name.

Sharkey spoke again.

"He's back. But you don't know, do you?"

"And what's your interest?"

"I need to find him. We have a mutual investment and I need his decision to act. And I need it now." *No point in saying that he had defrauded me of a large sum of money and then tried to kill me.*

"He left a trail of fraud behind him when he fled from here five years ago. And he stole my trust and undermined my good name. Yes, I'm a gambler. Always have been. But I'm an honest man. Everyone who has lost money to me knew the risk they were taking. I never defrauded them. But not Tommy. He wanted a short-cut to wealth. There is no short-cut. If he's back again he wouldn't risk coming near me. So, if you think that I can help you locate him, you're seriously mistaken."

Tom Gordon-Smith was totally believable. As belied a man who had excelled at poker. But he was not telling the truth. He'd known that his son was back in England. He'd known since the phone call he'd received shortly after Tommy had checked into the Cadogan Hotel. He shut up and looked directly at Sharkey. No need for an interpreter. The meeting was over. He was dismissed.

Jim Sharkey knew that he had hit a dead end. But it was still useful information. At least he wouldn't have to protect his back from the father. He did notice that one of the four men who had left the table had not moved away. He leaned against a pillar close to the table and easily within earshot of the conversation. He thought that that might be important. Or it might not. The man was now on his mobile phone and heading towards the door. He decided to follow. In his rush, he bumped into and almost knocked over a ghostly, waspish female figure. *Mousey, Mousey*, someone yelled as Sharkey steadied her and propped her against the bar. *What a beautifully ravaged face*, he thought, as he rushed out, afraid of losing the man he intended to follow.

Fifty-one

Following the man exercised all of Sharkey's skills. He had to follow without being seen. Up and down stairways and escalators, in and out of trains, crossing streets while staying in close pursuit. More than once he considered abandoning it, thinking that the chase was probably futile. Stubbornly, he stayed with it until they reached Stepney in London's East End. He walked the last half-mile to a street corner that said 'Jamaica St' and watched the man stop at the entrance to a modern apartment building. The man fired up a cigarette and waited, impatiently tapping from foot to foot. Sharkey merged into a doorway that sheltered him from view and waited too. In about ten minutes three other men joined the one he was following and they then entered the apartment building.

My gut tells me that this has got to be the place, Sharkey tells himself. *If I were a gambler, I'd bet that I've found Miller. Yeah, fucking Miller. The bastard will always be Miller to me. Calm down, calm down*, he told himself.

Sharkey waited in the doorway for thirty minutes until hunger pangs got the better of him. He decided that there was no guarantee that any of the men who entered the apartment building would re-appear any time soon. And, even if they did, the probability of them being accompanied by Tommy Gordon-Smith was remote. *So why am I hanging around,* he thought, *if Miller is indeed in there, then he wouldn't have been planning to leave any time soon. But when he hears the story about the American talking to his father, he will be spooked. Especially if they describe the American to him. But, hell, what am I saying: he won't know it's me. I'm dead! But he'll be spooked nevertheless. And he may flee. Find a hideout somewhere. I need to get him before he moves.*

He'd seen an Italian Restaurant at the corner of the street that he'd entered. It was an easy decision. And he'd still be close. He walked back to the intersection, saw the restaurant, crossed the street and went in. It had an Italian family ambiance and it was not busy. They seated him at a corner table with a good window view of the intersection. And very soon his *Tagliatelle Bolognese* arrived with a large glass of red and some fresh Italian bread straight out of the oven. It almost seduced Sharkey into making him forget why he was there. But he forced his mind back to reality. Lifting his eyes he watched the intersection, wondering if he was making a huge mistake.

Fifty-two

Tommy Gordon-Smith dragged four *Barney's Volcano* beers from the refrigerator, uncapped them and placed them on the breakfast counter-top. No need for glasses. *Bottle necks were the only thing that touched these guys' mouths,* he reminded himself.

"OK, Benny, start over and tell me again."

Benny Willis had a nervous twitch under his right eye. Tonight it was in top gear. He held the back of his fist to his eye, trying to stop the twitch. Failing, he picked up his beer, took a slug, and spoke, anxiety framing every word.

"It's like I said, Tommy. This American geezer pushed his way into our table. Looked at your dad and said he was looking for you."

He took another gulp of his beer. Deep breaths made him stop speaking again.

The Simms brothers stood side by side against the wall. Looking impassive, they could have passed as loyal retainers, bodyguards. But they were there to protect the interest of their crime boss uncle, Big Ned Simms. Wee Willie Richards slouched in the corner, a beer in his hand, untouched. Devious in his body language, with eyes that never looked directly, he was precision with a knife. Many of his better carvings had ended up in the Thames.

"Go on," prompted Tommy, having given Benny enough time to compose himself.

"Well, your old man asked us to leave the table while he talked to this jerk."

"So you don't know what he said."

"Yeah, I do. Bits and pieces anyway. I hung out close to them. The bar was noisy but I managed to get the drift of it. Seems this yank says that he knows you're here and that he wants to find you. Says you stole money from him. At least I think he said that."

He choked and coughed but somehow managed to keep on talking.

"Your father was mad as hell. Said he didn't give a damn about you. Said he had no son."

Tommy froze. He knew he'd left his father in the lurch five years ago when he fled. But he had planned to see him. Planned to make amends. This seemed to undermine any plans like that. His old man took no prisoners in life. And blood was not thicker in his book.

Benny was worried. Saw Tommy's reaction. Wished he'd never have said that. Tried to redeem himself.

"But I'm not sure, Tommy. The pub was noisy. I might have heard bad. And the yank was lookin' in my direction."

Tommy had regained his composure.

"What did this yank look like?"

"Och, Tommy, he was tall, about six feet, I think. Dark hair, combed straight back. Well built. Looked like he could handle himself. Didn't pay too much attention to his face. Good lookin', I'd say. Bushy eyebrows. I remember that."

Tommy's mind was in a whirl. *A yank who knows I'm in London. God, damn it, fuckin' Sharkey had bushy eyebrows. But he's gone. And I don't believe in ghosts. H-R must have connected me to their missing money. Maybe Sharkey left something. Something that pointed to me. That's it. That's got to be it. I should have had his apartment cleaned. I fucked up. Thought I was bullet-proof on this one. Fucking stupid!*

"What do you mean 'he was lookin' in your direction'?"

"I stayed back when the others left the table. I was leaning against a pillar near the table."

"And he fucking thought you were listening to them, didn't he?"

"Ough, I don't know, Tommy. That's when I left, called the boys and came here."

"Did he follow you?"

"Naw, naw! It's a long way from there and I watched my back. Nobody tailed me."

"Can you guarantee that?"

Benny tried to answer but the spittle began to gag him and he spluttered and coughed, ending up with,

"Aaagh, agh, Tommy …

"I can't assume that he didn't follow you. So I'll have to move. I have to move anyway. If there's one yank looking for me, I'm damn sure there will be more. And this is war."

Looking at the Simms brothers, he said,

"Tell Big Ned that I have a problem. And tell him to assemble the troops."

It was over. The Simms brothers left immediately. Benny hung back. Tommy turned and gave him a direct order.

"Make sure my wheels are in good shape. I'll be taking her out soon."

Benny left, reluctantly. He realized that Tommy did not want him around any longer.

Tommy had not touched his beer during the entire time. Now he picked it up, moved into the sitting room, sunk into a large well upholstered chair and lay back into two huge pillows. He needed time to consider his options. Needed time to figure out what was happening. Needed time to quietly think it through. Never one to get rattled easily, he admitted to himself that he had not anticipated this. Always felt so certain that he had covered his tracks very well. Did not think that they would trace Roger Coleman to Jack Miller to himself. So his first fear was irrational. This was a feat that called for the best. Certainly not that wimp Sharkey. And he trusted Bruce Morgan. If Bruce said he taken care of 'it', you could take that to the bank. So Sharkey is dead. And there's only one other option. Carlos and Eduardo have discovered that their money is missing. Always knew they would and figured that they'd want to keep a lid on it. Figured that they might eventually trace it to Sharkey. Hoped that if they did, they'd reach a dead end. But I was wrong. This yank must be working for them. Probably a skip/trace expert sent to find me. Find me so that H-R could dispose of me.

They can live with the lost money. But they could never live with the knowledge that I had taken them. No, they'll send in a hit team. And I must be ready for them. Expose them. Shine a light on them. There's more than one way to skin a cat.

Fifty-three

Jim Sharkey was using the bread to soak up the last of his *Tagliatelle Bolognese* sauce when his cell phone rang.

"I tried the house phone first before I tried your cell phone."

"Owen!"

"Out of sight, out of mind."

"Never! Not with your superb place branding your name in my head."

"Seriously, are you OK?"

"Yeah, just considered that this town is making me change to a lower gear."

"It'll do that. But it's all about to ratchet up. Maybe you should reconsider and get out of there. "

"If I don't find this bastard and confront him, I'll never be able to look myself in the face again."

"My sources tell me that the Pilkenroth twins are on their way to London. And I'm sure it's not a Pilkenroth business trip. We know they are contract killers for the global web spun by the remnants of ODESSA. But they're smart as hell, they're billionaires, and they're untouchable. Never leave any DNA at their crime scenes."

"Shit!"

"Yeah, they're deadly. You will not win if you go up against them."

"I'm hoping that they think I'm rotting in the Mojave. That gives me an advantage."

"Maybe. Maybe not. Any leads on Tommy Gordon-Smith?"

"Maybe. I went to Tom Senior's bookie joint in Camden. Claims he doesn't know where his son is. And he doesn't give a shit. Junior ripped him off five years ago and the old man does not forgive. But I followed a guy from there. I'm on his tail right now. I'm hoping that he'll lead me to Tommy."

"You have the equipment I left you?"

"Perfect. Snug fit."

"Use it if you have to. It's not traceable back to me."

"Owen, I owe you."

"Just get back in one piece. That will be payment enough."

Small talk was not their forte. Essentials done, the call ended. Sharkey had seen the twins' handiwork in Vegas and knew that their kind of hell would descend soon. He finished the last of his wine and found his patience rewarded. His quarry turned the corner walking with a slouch. Sharkey left a generous tip on the table and rushed out of the door in pursuit. Dusk was descending but the street lights still let him see well ahead. His brisk pace brought him within closing distance of his prey. *Yes. My prey. That's what I feel like. Wish he were Miller.* But he knew that letting his emotions get the better of him would cost him dearly. There were few people on the street and within a mile, his prey turned into a side street, less lighted than the main street. He looked over his shoulder and increased his pace. Sharkey knew he'd been spotted but there was insufficient light to let the guy recognize him, that is if he still remembered him from Tom Gordon-Smith's table at the pub in Camden. But he knew he must act soon. Or not at all. The street looked more industrial than residential. They soon reached a series of lock-up doors bordering the street. Looked like storage lock-ups or even garages. Sharkey merged into the shadows as the guy looked back and failed to see him. Sharkey watched him stop at the last door and fish for keys in his pockets. He found them but dropped them on the ground, knelt down and fished around for them. Got them, opened the lock, and slid the door open. Sharkey moved fast and forced his way into the lock-up before the guy could close the door. The guy backed up, afraid.

"Jesus! Get the fuck out of here!"

Sharkey had the Glock in his hand, holding it where the guy could see it.

"You know me, don't you?"

He moved into the shaft of light coming through a skylight window which glanced off the roof of a car. As his eyes adjusted to the light he could see that it was a Jag. As he moved closer, he could see that it wasn't any old Jag. It was an E-Type roadster. A collector's car.

He whimpered, "I don't know anything."

"Well, I think you do," said Sharkey, moving close to the man who had backed up into a corner with nowhere to go. He stuck the Glock in the man's midriff asking, "What's your name?"

"Benny....Benny Willis," said Benny, almost in a whimper.

"You know what I want, don't you Benny?"

"No, no ....no."

"Don't waste my time. You were in Joyce's pub with Tom Gordon-Smith when I asked him where I could find his son. You listened. Then you left. I followed you. I saw you go into that apartment building an hour ago."

"I'm only a mechanic. I fix cars. I don't know anything."

"Don't play dumb with me. Who owns this Jag?"

Sharkey emphasized his question by pushing the Glock into Benny's ribs. Afraid for his life, Benny talked.

"It's Tommy's car. I take care of it. Keep it in running condition in case he returns."

"And he's back, isn't he?"

Benny had lost his voice. He nodded his head as saliva drooled from the edge of his lips.

"And he's in that building. You met with him."

Eyes red and bleary, Benny nodded again.

"Who were the two other guys?"

"Big Ned's nephews."

"Big Ned?"

Benny knew he'd talked too much. But he was a coward. And, he thought, if Tommy is afraid of this fella, then it's OK for me to be afraid too. He cleared his throat and said.

"Big Ned Simms. Big Ned owns this town. Tommy owes him money. And he wants to be paid now. "

His eye had started to twitch again and that made him feel even more vulnerable. He realized that he'd said too much. Sharkey knew that that's all he would get from Benny. He felt that Big Ned was key. No point in hanging around the garage waiting for Tommy to appear. Better to find Big Ned and hang around there. Tommy was sure to show up soon. Big Ned didn't seem to be the type that would wait very long for his money.

"That's all I wanted to know. Wasn't that easy?"

He removed the Glock from Benny's ribcage. Benny held his ribs and started to walk away. But Sharkey blocked him and pointed the Glock at him,

"If Tommy knew you told me this, you'd be in big trouble, wouldn't you?" Benny nodded again.

"And you'll be in even bigger trouble with me if you say you've seen me. Understand?" Benny nodded again.

Fifty-four

London City Airport

Harvey bit his lower lip as they approached London City Airport. The steep glide path turned his knuckles white but he hid all that from Howard who had a huge grin on his face. A ceiling of clear blue skies over the Thames created a perfect canvas for The London Eye, the Houses of Parliament and Big Ben, as they flew over Canary Wharf and eased down onto the runway, which sat between the Royal Albert and the King George V docks. As the wheels hit, Harvey relaxed his hands and Howard punched the air in exhilaration.

A limousine driver awaited them at arrivals. A small rotund man with puffy cheeks and inquisitive eyes, he wore a dark blue chauffer's uniform and a soft peaked cap, and held a large white sign with *Pilkenroth* in black. They strode directly to him and he welcomed them with a friendly cockney greeting:

"Name's *Arfur*. Welcome ter London."

The twins thanked him and followed him to the limousine. He took their bags and put them in the trunk.

"Beautiful day, innit?" he said, as he ushered them into the limo. Behind the wheel, he looked back at them and confirmed the address: a mews house in Belgravia.

"Belgravia ain't far. Know what I mean?"

Traffic moved briskly and, true to their driver's word, they soon pulled up in front of the mews house in a quiet street in Belgravia. One side of the street was all mews houses and theirs stood in the centre. The keys had been dispatched to them, by overnight courier, before they left the States. Horst Richter had explained that it was one of H-R International's executive lodgings in London. He also explained that this one was their *safe house*.

The driver and limo belonged to H-R so the twins didn't have to fumble for change. Nevertheless, Harvey insisted that Arthur take the £50 tip that he squeezed into his hand with a brief thanks. *Arfur's* face broke into a beatific smile and he tipped his hat and bowed to the twins. Harvey had just bought *Arfur's* loyalty.

They tossed a coin to choose the between the two bedrooms. Harvey won. He was always lucky. Even at the gambling tables in Vegas. He chose the bedroom that looked out over a large green space (too large to be called a garden) bordered with a variety of trees and shrubs; it was the back of the large mansion house to the rear. Once, in the distant past, this mews house was used to stable their horses. Hubert had to settle for the other room, whose window looked directly into the brick walls of the large townhouses on the opposite side of the street.

They dropped their bags, unopened, in their bedrooms and avoided the wine rack as they squeezed through the kitchen to a closet door set in the wall. Opening the door, they lifted the carpet square on the closet floor to reveal a metal ring embedded in the floor. Harvey pulled it and the closet floor lifted to expose a metal staircase that circled downwards.

Hubert said what they both felt:

"Brilliant"

"A secret 19th century passageway. A connection to the big house."

"And they had many salacious secrets."

Their laughter reverberated around the stairwell as they descended. A light switch on the wall illuminated the passage below. But there was no passage. It had been blocked off. A steel door with a combination lock and two regular locks sat flush against the wall that had blocked the passage. Hubert pulled the keys he'd been sent from his pocket, located the two keys that would unlock the door. They did. Then he looked at the slip of paper in his wallet where he had the numbers that would open the combination lock. He entered them and they could hear the lock release. A louder sliding click due to the closed space. Hubert lifted the handle and the door swung open to reveal a large equipment room. An armory. But more than that. It held survival suits, scuba diving equipment, bullet proof vests, steel cutters, and much more. But the equipment that Hubert and Harvey wanted filled a large cabinet on the rear wall. Every kind of weapon was there. They wondered. *Might they have our favorites? Yes, yes!* Huge grins spread ear to ear as they retrieved a Walther P-38 and a Browning P-35 High Power. Harvey said:

"Can't be a coincidence?"

"They know what we use. We've worked long enough for Carlos. It's no coincidence."

As they climbed back up the stairs, Harvey quipped: "Maybe they know the wines we like to drink."

Halfway into an excellent *Cloudy Bay* sauvignon blanc they had found in the refrigerator, Harvey's cell phone rang.

"Horst, yes we expected your call."

"You have seen our tool shed?"

"Love it. Got our favorite tools. Thank you."

Preliminaries aside, Horst got right to the point.

"Carlos told you what I want."

"Terminate. With extreme prejudice."

"Exactly."

"But we have to find him first."

"He's in London but we don't know where. We do know where his father is. Tom Gordon-Smith is well known. Owns a chain of bookie shops."

"And you're suggesting?"

"I'm not suggesting anything. But if you can't find him, you can always make him come to you."

Horst gave Harvey the location of Tom Gordon-Smith's flagship joint, G-S Bookmakers, in Camden Town. He also gave them his home address in Hampstead.

Fifty-five

Paraguay

Carlos was preparing to return to Miami when the phone call came in from London. Expecting to find either Hubert or Harvey on the line, he answered, eagerly awaiting an update.

"Didn't expect to hear from you so soon."

"Thought I was that thug you sent to get me, didn't you, Carlos?"

The voice was unmistakable.

"You're a dead man, Roger!"

"Who are you to talk to me? You're a criminal. Your company is built on the bodies of the dead. Built on the treasures stolen by the SS. That's your legacy, Carlos!"

Carlos refused to be baited.

"And to think that you might have wed my sister! You're a con-man, a thief, and a criminal. Thought you could rob me and get away with it. Did you? Did you? Did you?"

"Robbery! Hah! Consider it my severance package. It's small compensation for losing Elena."

"You'll never live to spend it. You're a dead man."

"Shooting from the hip, as usual. Aren't you forgetting my insurance policy?"

Carlos was now on high alert. *The bastard is threatening me*, he thought.

"Are you threatening me?"

"Simply advising you that you will bring down your own house of cards if you've given your agent in London orders to take me out."

"Fuck you, Roger! You're a dead man! Do you hear me? A dead man!"

"Then you're committing suicide. Don't you think that I would have taken out an insurance policy when I worked at H-R?"

Better call this bastard's bluff, thought Carlos.

"Once a con-man, always a con-man. You can't bluff me."

"No bluff. What would happen if I told the world about the billions that H-R has laundered through Abu Dhabi and Oman?"

Carlos still felt that Coleman was bluffing. No-one in general management knew anything about the ODESSA funds that H-R laundered through the middle east. *No way could Coleman have known,* Carlos assured himself.

"All our middle east business is open and transparent. We operate within all agreed banking and legal regulations. No one lays the sins of their fathers at the feet of this generation. It won't sell. No one will buy."

"Carlos, when the press sees the evidence I have, it will sell. Big Time! So you'd better keep me alive."

With that, he hung up on Carlos.

Carlos poured himself a Jameson and sat down. He suddenly felt tired. But he had to make a decision. Had to toss a coin. Had to take a gamble. Was Coleman bluffing? Or did he really have the evidence he speaks about. *That's the heart of the matter,* contemplated Carlos. He's a con man. A good one. Chances are he's bluffing. I have to go with that. Time to call the twins, he decided. He dialed Hubert's cell and got through to him in London.

"I need an update."

"Nothing yet, Carlos."

"What do you mean? You've found him, right?"

"No, no, we haven't. But we'll get him."

"Hey, something doesn't add up here."

"What do you mean?"

"He called me. The audacious bastard just called me from London. Threatened me. Told me that I had *sent a thug to get him.* Told me to lay-off or he'd ensure that the press would get some derogatory shit about H-R."

"It's not us. He said *a thug.* One thug? Couldn't be us. Wait a minute. What about your colleague Horst. Maybe he's sent one of his contractors in. Hedging his bets."

Carlos considered that. Just like something Horst would do. And never admit it either.

"Get that bastard and get him now. I don't care what you need to do. Flush him out. Find a way."

Harvey waited pensively while Hubert was on the phone. He could feel the tension in the air. The virtue of being a twin.

Always. Referred pain. Referred joy. And referred tension today. Hubert's face was grim at the end of the call.

"There's somebody else trying to fill our contract."

He then filled Harvey in on his conversation with Carlos.

"We've never shared a contract with anyone. And we're not going to this time."

"If we can't find our man, then we need to make him come to us."

They knew what they needed to do. And they knew they needed to move on it.

Fifty-six

Dania, Florida

Carlos had flown into Miami International from Asuncion and was now on route I95 headed for Dania. Traffic jostled for place and position on the overcrowded highway. Carlos knew that he could never live as these people did, fighting their way up I95 every morning. Already he was feeling depleted. He felt happy that Eduardo ran their Dania bank. It wouldn't have suited him at all. But he had to have a 'one-on-one' with Eduardo. The 'family' gatherings in Asuncion divided them more than united them. Carlos knew that this was a critical time. Perhaps the most critical time that their family and their business had faced in recent years. And a threat to the legacy that they had inherited.

Coleman's threat, if carried out, could undermine everything they stood for, cripple their ability to fund the efforts and people who shared their legacy and their view of the future. He needed to find out if Coleman could have acquired the documentation that would enable him to carry out his threat. Or, preferably, to ensure himself that Coleman was bluffing. That would be true to character for a conman and gambler like Coleman. But he had to make sure.

He swung into the bank's parking lot, got out and stretched his legs. Palm trees bordered the lot and bougainvillea climbed over the wire fencing, dispelling the harsh scenery on I95.

Eduardo was expecting him. Double glass doors opened into the executive office suite. Victoria, Eduardo's PA, greeted Carlos as he entered and took him to Eduardo's office. Eduardo stood up from his large walnut desk, walked around to Carlos and escorted him to a comfortable seat at the circular glass table in the center of the office. Carlos looked ill at ease.

He said, "The damn flight hit turbulence. Lots of it. I hate that."

Eduardo grimaced at that. Carlos continued,

"I hope it's not a portent of things to come."

"You seemed to be in a panic when you called and you wouldn't tell me what caused it."

"I couldn't talk over the phone."

At that moment, almost as though it were arranged to pause the conversation, Eduardo's secretary arrived with coffee and croissants.

"Figured you would need your morning coffee," quipped Eduardo, trying to ease the tension he sensed in Carlos. As Chairman and CEO of the bank, he was frequently faced with tension he had to dissipate and fires he had to quench.

Carlos did indeed relax a little. The morning coffee, an addiction, always had that effect on him. Finally Carlos briefed Eduardo on the matter that he couldn't discuss over the phone, the Coleman threat. Eduardo had assumed that the Coleman issue and the theft of their funds had been taken care of by Carlos. No news he assumed was good news. So he looked at Carlos and said,

"But I thought this had all been taken care of…"

"Unfortunately, no. Coleman was behind the theft at MetroBank. He set up some patsy, some failed banker called Sharkey to do the dirty work and then managed to get rid of him. His bones have been picked clean by vultures out in the Mojave. Thought we'd reach a dead end. But he fucked up. Left too many trails behind him. I hired the twins for the job."

"The Pilkenroths. They are more dangerous than they're worth. Are you sure that was a good idea."

"You're right. They are bloodthirsty. But they are loyal. And remember, Horst asked for 'blood' on this one. And I intend to give it to him."

"So where are the twins now?"

"They're in London. To wrap this up. But the bastard is clever. He's evaded us so far. And then has the audacity to call and threaten me! But the twins will get him. I just want to make sure that he didn't acquire any evidence here that will help him carry out his threat."

"He was only here for a couple of months. Sporadically. Whenever he could break away from Elena. It was easy to trot up here from Miami whenever he liked. We're all guilty. He was a charming bastard. And Elena loved him. So we wanted to find a place for him in the business."

"So what did he do when he was here?"

"I assigned him to three members of our top management team. Take him around. Orient him. Branches, back office, data processing, finance and treasury. And he sat in on a number of our board meetings."

"So he couldn't have gained access to any information about our special client relationships?"

"No. No way! No-one can access any of that. Not our internal audit team. Not the National Bank examiners."

"The Fed audits you regularly?"

"Yes. The Federal Reserve, the FDIC (Federal Deposit Insurance Corporation, the OCC (Office of the Controller of the Currency). We are audited and regulated on everything from capital adequacy to customer risk. We do our own internal audits, monthly, quarterly, spot checks too. We cannot allow ourselves to be embarrassed by receiving a poor rating from the Fed."

"So it's obvious that none of the data on the special relationships that we manage can be uncovered by any audit or examination."

"Correct."

"So Coleman could not have anything in his possession that could harm us?"

"No. I don't see how he could."

"What about our correspondent bank relationships? Our funds transfers?"

"All conform to regulations."

"But we know otherwise, don't we?"

"But all such funds are clean at source before they enter our network."

"Other than yourself, does anyone else know?"

Eduardo looked troubled when he was asked that. He considered before answering.

"Only one person. Our head of security, our very own cousin."

Carlos almost choked on the name, "Hector Ramirez."

"Yes."

"And Hector died in that speedboat crash."

"Yes. Since then I am the only one who has access to information on our special clients."

"Was Hector one of the management team you assigned to Coleman's orientation?"

"Yes, he was. But he would never have divulged anything to Coleman."

Eduardo tried to say that with total assurance. But it fell flat. Carlos got up and walked around the office. At the window, he turned back and looked at Eduardo.

"But it's not a sure bet, is it. So Coleman may be bluffing. But what if he's not?"

They decided that Eduardo would scrub the bank of any sign whatsoever of their special clients or the less than clean funds that they laundered on their behalf. Carlos left, hoping that Coleman, being the consummate gambler and conman, was bluffing this time.

As Carlos prepared to leave, Eduardo said, "Are you going to see Elena?"

"I'm not welcome, am I?"

"She won't see me. But I think you have to try."

"Convince me."

"I think she's depressed. She has been in Ibiza with her Murphy friends. I called her when she returned. But she wasn't interested in seeing me. I'll try again. But I think you should go there before you leave Miami. Don't call. Don't ask. Just go."

"She knows nothing about the real Coleman and that he robbed us of eight million. Does she?"

"No. She knows none of that."

"Should I tell her?"

"You'll have to be the judge of that."

"What do you think?"

"I don't know. Maybe she should know. Show her how lucky she is to have escaped from this man."

They parted on that note and Carlos took the elevator down to the car park. The Miami sun shone relentlessly from the sky. He donned his sunglasses, clicked his keys and the car doors opened. But as soon as he touched the steering wheel, he thought that it would burn him. Felt like an oven inside. He rolled down all the windows and waited until it cooled enough to let him drive.

Traffic on I95 was as thick and angry as usual. Most drivers seemed driven by impatience and anxiousness. They constantly tried to squeeze in and out of any available space on any lane, attempting to gain ground. A futility. But it satisfied their anxiety. Carlos stayed in the slow lane, letting them move in and out of the rare space that opened in front of him. *Survival of the fittest* came to mind, but here he thought it was *survival of the unfit*.

It was a relief when, thirty minutes later, he showed his security card at the gate and was waved through. He eased the car into Elena's driveway, got out and walked to her front door. He stood in the middle of her doorway, positioned to let the camera capture him, and rang the bell. If she was home, she'd see him. Whether she decided to let him in or not was her choice. He was patient. He'd wait and see.

Elena wasn't expecting anyone. *Probably a sales call or maybe the Jehovah's Witnesses again. They do persist. Even though I've told them numerous times that I don't believe a word of it.*

She looked at the security camera and saw Carlos. Now she was faced with a dilemma. *Should I let him in or should I ignore him? The Murphys would advise me to face everything. Face it and put it behind me.*

She opened the door and let him in. Carlos saw her as he crossed the entrance hall and thought she looked good. Fit and healthy looking. *Ibiza must have treated her well,* he thought.

He moved to greet her with a kiss but she shunned that and said,

"What brings you here?"

"I had to see you. I don't want us to be enemies."

"Well, you treated me like one."

"Elena, I did not intend to do that. Coleman was the enemy. Not you. But I guess I can see how you might look at it that way."

"Damn right, Carlos. On my wedding day. And you didn't even try to break the news to me. Just let me suffer. You chose to make an enemy of me."

"Well, I came here to say I'm sorry. And to ask you to forgive me. I know it's a big ask."

Elena simply stared at him, no expression on her face. So Carlos continued:

"I was trying to protect you."

"No, you were trying to protect the family. No, not even the family, just the Himmler-Ramos brand!"

"But you are the family, Elena. Don't you know that?"

Once again, Elena stared at him, expressionless.

"You are a very lucky person."

"You'd better explain that."

Carlos had decided to tell her everything.

"Your Roger was a fraud and a criminal. His real name is Tommy Gordon-Smith. A common thief. He never went back to England. Got off the plane in Atlanta and disappeared. Used another phony name in New York. Jack Miller. Conned a banker into stealing eight million dollars of our international wire transfers. Had him killed and dumped in the Mojave. That's your brilliant Roger Coleman!"

Carlos had rattled all of this off in almost one sentence. He realized that he might as well have hit Elena over the head. He could see the color drain from her face and her hands seeking a prop to steady herself. He rushed and caught her as she fainted into his arms.

Carlos stayed with Elena for the next two days. Stayed till he was sure she had recovered from the shock. Stayed till he saw evidence that she had finally realized how lucky she had been to escape the clutches of Roger Coleman.

Fifty-seven

London

Tommy Gordon-Smith walked to the drinks cabinet where he closed his fist around the neck of a bottle of Oban single malt. His favorite scotch. He knew he shouldn't but he poured a generous helping into his whisky glass. Glass in right hand, he sank into the sitting-room couch. He was losing control. He felt paranoid and then admonished himself. *Not me*, he thought, *not me*. But the walls were closing in on him. Big Ned was shaking him down for more and he did not like the big man's nephews dogging him wherever he went. And now H-R had connected him to their missing money, something he was sure he'd covered up well, something he was sure would lead them to Sharkey and a blind alley.

But I fucked up, he said, out loud.

And now they've sent a hit man to take me out. Carlos knew they'd sent a hit man. He didn't admit it. But he didn't deny it either. So the contact must have been issued in Zurich. Horst! He had met Horst once at H-R's Miami headquarters and hated him instantly. His inherited hatred of Nazi Germany made him distrust all Germans. He felt that they still intended to take over the world. But why an American hit man? Why not a European? Guess it's a global profession.

So the bastard Horst has sent a man to kill me.

He put the bottle away. Couldn't afford to get drunk. He needed to go on the offensive. Couldn't wait. He knew what he needed to do.

I'll pay off Big Ned and ask for protection.
Then I'll go public with the H-R laundering stuff.
That'll give them more to worry about than me.
We'll track this hit man. Big Ned will take him out.
And Horst? Yes, Horst? The Nazi fucker!
I'll have to think about that!

Fifty-eight

Hampstead, London

The twins exited the Hampstead Heath Overground Station at exactly nine pm – late enough to beat the rush hour traffic and the right time of day to execute their mission. They were dressed in gym attire, casual clothing that allowed them to blend. Harvey carried a gym back-pack, large enough to accommodate all their special equipment. Their destination, Tom Gordon-Smith Sr's home, stood about five-hundred meters away, across the road from Hampstead Heath. A quiet, up-market neighborhood. Harvey couldn't resist:

"Good pubs in the village."

"And you think we'll be able to drop in on one?"

"Why not? This might be an easy gig."

"Don't get lulled into thinking like that. Just because this neighborhood seems so civilized doesn't mean it holds no threat. We don't need a fight with the local cops. Don't know if we'd win that one."

"Hey, we beat these Brits in 1776!"

"Come on, Harvey, don't be so fuckin' silly."

Harvey burst into one of his laughing spurts, the kind that invaded him like hiccups, the kind of broken laughter that he could not stop. Hubert punched him on the shoulder but that only made Harvey double over in splutters.

"Shit, Harvey, you weren't that funny. Save it. You'll need it when all this is over."

The thought of their mission sobered Harvey. He suddenly stopped laughing. He knew the levity was a cover-up. He had a bad premonition about this gig,

"Are you sure he's alone?"

"As sure as I can be. You got the same info that I did. Wife died a year ago. Cancer. One daughter, three grand-kids, lives in Wembley. She hates him. Never sees him."

"Yeah, but he might have company."

"He has one late night poker game in his house. Wednesdays. And it gets cancelled if he has business to attend to. Business takes precedent. He's a man of order, discipline."

"You got all that from that one phone call?"

"You listened to it, didn't you?"

"Yeah. But you stayed on the call after you turned off the speaker phone."

"So you're accusing me of keeping stuff from you!"

"No, no!"

"Well..."

"Come on, it's just that I have a bad feeling about this gig tonight."

"You've been spooked. Not like you. You never get spooked. What's up?"

"Nothing I can put my finger on. It's this damn town. There's something surreal about it. Tidy, mannered veneer that somehow seems false. Almost like thin ice. And tonight I'm beginning to see cracks in it."

"Shit, Harvey! Cut it out, drama queen! That's bullshit and you know it. This is a job like any other. And don't we live for the challenge, the adrenalin rush. No amount of money can buy this for us!"

Harvey didn't answer that. He had no answer. They were close to Tom Gordon-Smith's house and they could see one dim light illuminating the curtain in the front room. A fanlight over the door threw a small shaft of light over the entrance.

They crossed the street and walked past the house but they did not see inside. The light in the room cast an opaque glow through the curtain. Beyond the house, they stopped to discuss tactics.

"We need to get invited in. He'll disarm his security to do that. So it's best if you get the invite," said Hubert.

"What do you mean?"

"You're the friendliest looking one. It's that simple. I'll stay away from the door. We have to assume that he has a front door security camera."

"OK. But what's my script? Am I selling encyclopedias door-to-door?"

"Come on, Harvey. That's not funny."

"Ease up, Hubie! I know what to do. We can't fool this old guy. I'll be honest. I'll tell him I'm looking for his son. I'll tell him that his son is in big trouble. I'll tell him that I'm a friend from the States. And that I need to find his son to warn him. How about that?"

"Good, very good. Believable. Go for it."

Hubert stayed hidden as Harvey rang the door bell and waited. No answer. He rang again. And waited a little longer this time. Still no answer. Frustrated and impatient, he looked at Hubert to see what he thought. But Hubert simply nodded his head, confirming that he should try again. So he rang again, a more prolonged ring this time.

Inside Tom Gordon-Smith heard the first ring and ignored it. He didn't want to be bothered. He was watching Chelsea, his favorite football team in action. Only one goal ahead and they were under huge pressure. Then the doorbell rang a second time, more insistent it seemed. He turned down the volume on the TV and went to the hallway to look at the picture on the security camera. He saw a round faced, young man with the semblance of a smile, rocking gently back and forth as though he was listening to music. *Pretty innocuous looking,* he thought. *I'll ignore him and maybe he'll go away.* But halfway back to his game, the doorbell rings again, more demanding this time. He swore under his breath. *Ignoring this prick won't make him go away. He looks a little simple minded. I'll have to speak to him.*

"Yes?"

"Mr. Gordon-Smith?"

"Yes, what do you want?"

"I need to see you. It's very important. It's about your son."

The American accent was obvious. Another one. He clearly remembered the one who had approached him in Joyce's. Gave off threatening vibes. But this guy, with his big friendly smile, does not seem threatening."

"What about my son?"

"He's a friend and he's disappeared. He's in a lot of trouble and I need to reach him. Can I come in to speak to you about it?"

Tom knows that he must hear what this guy has to say. Two Americans looking for his son, all in the same week. Too much of a coincidence. He walks back to the hallway bureau, slides out the bottom drawer, removes his gun and sticks it in his belt at the back. Near enough to reach quickly. And not too obvious to frighten off this guy. *Ok, let me play this thing out and see what happens.*

He walks back to the intercom and answers.

"Ok, I'm going to let you come in to talk with me. But you better not be conning me!"

Tom disarmed his security, opened the front door and invited the man in – but just as he crossed the threshold, a second man, a double, pushed his way through, holding a weapon pointed directly at him. Tom considered pulling his gun but never got the chance. They backed him up through the hallway back into the living room. Hubert held him while Harvey searched him and removed the gun.

Tom is angry. Angry at himself for his own stupidity. He shouts, "What kind of a game are you playing? What do you want? I told your mate in Joyce's pub that I didn't know anything."

But they said nothing. Forced him to sit down in the couch while they turned off the TV and closed the heavy drapes across the front window. Then they settled in the two chairs facing him. This time Hubert spoke.

"We have no mates. Your son stole eight million dollars from the company he worked for. They want their money back. We've been contracted to fulfil that. And we aim to do it."

"Your mate came to me with some story about an investment with Tommy that was at risk. I didn't believe him. Why should I believe you?"

"Whoever saw you is no mate of ours. But you can believe us. We are not leaving here until your son walks in that door with the money."

Hubert stood up, crossed to the side table, picked up the phone, and handed it to Tom.

"Call your son. Now!"

"I don't know where he is."

"We believe you do."

"You're wasting your time."

"Mr. Gordon-Smith, let me assure you. We do not waste time. I'll put it to you bluntly. If we leave here without the money, I guarantee you that your son will be an orphan. And we'll still get him."

Tom prized himself on reading faces. He would not have been so successful at poker without such an inherent skill. And now he believed this man, Hubert. *A dangerous psychopath if I ever saw one*, he thought, *and what guarantee do I have that he won't take the money and kill Tommy too.*

"What guarantee do I have that you won't take the money and kill Tommy too?"

"Our client wants this matter to be solved with no publicity. Why do you think they never reported this to the police? We intend to blacklist your son on every credit bureau and on every financial market in the world. All his credit cards will be withdrawn. That will be sufficient punishment, don't you think?"

Hubert could see that Tom Gordon-Smith wanted to believe this. *I can play poker too,* thought Hubert, *my contract is for termination with extreme prejudice and I will lie through my teeth if necessary.* He watched Tom's body language and could see him reach acceptance before he spoke.

"I will contact him. You give me no choice. But, let me warn you. If you lay a finger on him, you will not leave this country alive."

Hubert believed that Tom believed what he had said. And he knew that he must have a sense of control to enable him to proceed. He watched him dial the phone,

"I want to speak to Ned. No, I'll hold. Tell him it's very important."

He waited with the phone to his ear, never looking at Hubert and Harvey.

"Ned…yeah, it's a goddamn situation. Two American fuckers are holding me at gun-point, insisting that they speak to Tommy. Say he's ripped off their client. Big bucks. I don't know exactly where he is but you do. Have him call me back."

Fifty-nine

Tommy tried to rouse himself from his slumber. Something had awakened him but he didn't know what. A voice on the phone. That's it. But soon the ringing of the phone penetrated his head again. *Fucking persistent*, he swore to himself, as he lumbered off the couch and reached the phone.

"Yeah!"

"Tommy, it's me. Ned. Are you OK?"

"Sure. Been catching forty winks, that's all."

"Well, listen up. You've got big, big trouble."

Ned than filled him in on the call he'd received from his father. As Tommy listened he got angrier and angrier. He couldn't contain his anger.

"The bastards. The scum. Hired guns from H-R, the company I worked for. They're a bunch of fucking ex-Nazis, Ned. Yeah, I relieved them of some coins. Enough to pay you back and give myself a fresh start. It's dirty money, anyway."

"Your dad isn't easily conned or threatened. But he sounds like he's in a lot of trouble. These bastards, as you call them, want you to call them back. They're holding your dad hostage at his home until they hear from you. You call them and then call me back. Your dad and I go back a long way, Tommy. Anybody hurts him hurts me. I'll get a couple of my boys."

Still ferociously angry, Tommy heads for the bathroom and soaks his head under the shower. He pops two paracetamol tablets into his mouth. Looking at the open whiskey bottle on his return to the living room, he's tempted to raise it to his lips. *But that kind of dutch courage is not what I need*, he tells himself, *now I need a cool head.*

He picks up the phone and calls his dad.

"Tommy, they gave me no choice. They want their money back."

Just then, Harvey pulled the phone away and handed it to Hubert.

"You've been a bad boy, Roger. Or maybe you're Jack. But you're really Tommy. A man of many parts, aren't you, Tommy?"

"Who the fuck are you?"

"Carlos is very unhappy with you, Tommy."

"Let my father go and we can settle this."

"Oh, no. As I told your father, you come here with the money you stole or, when we leave here, you will be an orphan."

"You're a sick fuck."

"Oh, no, Tommy. We're in fine health."

"How do I know you only want the money. It doesn't ring true to me."

"Think about it. Carlos would love to kill you. Better yet, he'd love to torture you and watch you experience a very slow agonizing death. I know that. And that's what you'd expect, wouldn't you? But you forget that Carlos is the face of a huge multinational corporation. He can't afford to do what he'd like to. So he wants his money back. And he's going to black-ball you in every financial and credit window on this planet. But – and listen well – we love this stuff and we don't mind spilling blood. So, just give us an opportunity and we'll fulfil those desires of ours. Don't co-operate and we'll settle for your dad's blood instead."

"I admit. You've got me. I'll bring the money there. And I want you to let my father go when I arrive."

"Don't take too long, Roger, I mean Tommy. And do come alone. We hate collateral damage. We detest it."

Felling grim and cornered, but resolute, Tommy got off the phone. He reflected back on his earlier thoughts: *H-R can live with the lost money. But they could never live with the knowledge that I had taken them. No, they'll send in a hit team. And I must be ready for them. Expose them. Shine a light on them. There's more than one way to skin a cat.*

Then he called Big Ned and filled him in.

"I'm going to bring some money with me. You'll have to wait a while for your next half mill."

"That's not a priority, Tommy. Saving your dad is. There's four of us. We're going with you."

"They told me to come alone."

"Of course they did. Did they believe you would?"

"I don't know."

"If my hunch is right, they'll be hedging their bets. In case you didn't come alone."

"OK. I'll get the money and drive to your place."

"You think the money is all they want?"

"No. They want me dead. I'm sure of that. But I've got to get my dad."

"Alright, when you get here, we'll decide how we want to handle it."

Tommy opened the door to his lock-up, unlocked the floor safe and put the entire mill and a half in a large black expandable case. *I'll buy them off or distract them with this,* he told himself. Knowing that it really wouldn't work. *But maybe it'll give Big Ned and his boys an edge.* That's all we need. He searched deeper in the floor safe and retrieved a package of documents and two thumb drives; his security he had once thought. But now it might very well be his legacy. He had already packaged and stamped it for mailing to the managing editor at the *Times.* Payback. He'd prove to Carlos that he wasn't bluffing.

He sat in his Jaguar running his hands over the smooth steering wheel, letting it soothe and strengthen him. Then he started the engine, pulled out of the lock-up and drove back to his apartment building. Stopping briefly, he ran inside and gave the package to the concierge, telling him to mail it immediately. He jumped in his jag again and headed for Big Ned Simms house.

Sixty

Wapping, London

Jim Sharkey parked his brand new rented Ford Escort across the street from Big Ned Simms' house in Wapping. It wasn't hard to find. The little Escort was remarkably fast and superbly maneuverable. The exact combination for managing the streets of London. He'd stuffed a rug, a pillow, a couple of sandwiches, and a bottle of coke in the back. He could feel the Glock in its holster and it added an edge, giving him the same feeling that he had in the Gulf before a firefight. He didn't know how long his stakeout would be. But he intended to stay. He believed that Tommy would be here soon.

Forty-five minutes later, Jim sat up straight and took his iPad earphones out. A black limo had pulled up outside Big Ned's house. Looked like a Daimler. Three men jumped out and rushed towards the front door. They were admitted immediately.

Twenty minutes later, Tommy's Jaguar pulled in behind the Daimler. Tommy got out and went inside.

Wish I could be a fly on the wall in there, thought Sharkey, *something big is going down. I can feel it in my bones.*

Whatever it was, it didn't take long. Thirty minutes later, the three men accompanied by Big Ned, emerged and got into the Daimler. They were all carrying various weapons. Looked as though this was perfectly normal. *I guess if you are a gang leader like Big Ned it would be perfectly normal,* observed Sharkey to himself. Tommy trailed behind and got into his Jag. Sharkey turned the key in his ignition and readied his Escort. He knew he had to follow them.

Despite almost losing them a couple of times, lights and traffic worked on his behalf, slowing them enough to allow him to keep up. Finally they reached Hampstead Heath and their destination, Tom Gordon-Smith's house. Sharkey had done his homework. He knew this was where Tommy's father lived. The mystery deepened for him. He couldn't figure out why they had all arrived here. And armed.

Some shit is happening, he reckoned. He parked the Escort within view of the house and watched as Tommy got out of his Jag and approached the house carrying an attaché case. Big Ned got out of the Daimler and joined him. They both approached the front door and waited. Minutes passed while they stood there. Finally they pushed the door and it opened. It was obviously unlocked. Sensing a trap, they hesitated. But only for a moment. Then they both went inside. At the same time, the other three men left the Daimler, carrying their weapons and approached the house. Two circled around the back and one positioned himself outside the front door.

Lightning struck Sharkey: *it's the twins! why didn't I think of that right away, bet they're holding the old man captive!*

Sixty-one

Hampstead, London

Tom Gordon-Smith's door had been left open in anticipation. Tommy entered the hallway first, closely followed by Big Ned who carried a gun in his right hand. He wanted to let them know that they faced a fight. *Transparency can make people think* was a favorite of Big Ned's. But he didn't know the twins. And that was his mistake.

The hallway was dark, unlit. Light showed through the glass in the door that connected them to the living room. They hesitated. But they had no choice. They must confront these people. They pushed the door. It was already open and now it opened wide. Tom sat in a high-backed armchair with a reading lamp directed at him. The rest of the room was dim, barely illuminated at all.

"I told you to come alone, didn't I?"

Tommy peered in the direction of the voice. He could see a dark outline of a man seated directly opposite his father and looking straight at him.

"Well, I don't trust you. I didn't believe you."

"And now you expect me to trust you?"

"I don't give a fuck! I came here for one reason. To get my father. I want you to release him now. Now! Before we negotiate a thing."

"But we had no plans to negotiate Tommy. You must know that."

"I don't care what Carlos told you. I called him myself. And he knows that, if anything happens to me, I will release information that will bring his house down."

"Oh, Tommy, Tommy, as though I care."

"I have a couple of million in this attaché case. We walk away and it's all yours. Keep it. You don't have to tell Carlos."

"Oh, Tommy, how naïve you are. What's a couple of million mean to us? Surely you know that."

At that exchange, Big Ned moved further into the light with his drawn gun.

"My men have this house surrounded and if you start anything you will never leave here alive. Tom is my friend and I want you to release him now. That's not negotiable."

A sudden burst of maniacal laughter erupted from Hubert. Followed by the flash of a gun. Big Ned clutched his chest, buckled at the knees, and fell face down on the floor in his own blood, already starting to stain the carpet beneath him. Shots rang out from the rear of the house and they could hear Harvey join in the laughter. The man at the front door rushed in, gun drawn, and fell. A bullet added a third eye to his face and removed the back of his skull on its way out.

Tommy ran to his father, pulled him out of the chair, and turned towards the door when the lights went up. Frozen like a rabbit in a car's headlight, he stood transfixed. Hubert looked directly at him.

"A futility, Tommy. You were right. Carlos doesn't care about the money. He wants blood!"

Hubert levelled his weapon at him and pulled the trigger just as Tommy's father leaped in front of him, taking the bullet intended for his son. Tommy knew his father was dead before he hit the floor. He had no choice but to run. He ran into the darkened hallway as the bullets smashed into the wall on either side of him.

Sixty-two

Hampstead, London

His father dead, and Big Ned dead too, Tommy hit the street running. He'd failed to save his father and now he had to save himself.

Thinking that the best approach would be to hide in plain sight, he avoided his Jaguar and ran towards the village. Seeing no-one follow, he slows to a walk, sure to be less conspicuous that way. He walks directly into the village. He remembers his favourite pub, *The Duke of Hamilton*. He was here before. Five years ago. He and Gemma used to hang out here. *Another lifetime,* he chided himself. *I suppose her name still haunts me. Especially since the lady who collapsed in* The Bunch of Grapes *looked so much like her...*

Sharkey had been waiting in his car, wondering what was happening in the house. Whatever it was, it was all over in twenty minutes. One of Big Ned's men rushed out from behind the house, jumped into the Daimler, and took off at breakneck speed. Almost immediately, Tommy left the house running, his large case slung over his shoulder. Sharkey knew he had to follow. He ran after Tommy, keeping him in sight but not alerting him. Soon Tommy slowed to a walk as he neared the village. He watched him enter *The Duke of Hamilton.* Sharkey followed.

The pub was crowded. Locals out for a social evening. Others for a late meal. *All very civilized,* thought Sharkey. Tommy pushed up against the bar, ordered a pint, and took it to one of the few empty seats at a tall round table in the corner.

Sharkey decided. It's now or never.

He strode purposefully toward Tommy, who seemed to be sitting, head lowered, sipping his pint, not wanting to meet or talk with anyone. *Post traumatic stress,* thought Sharkey, *saw enough of that in the Gulf. I'd recognize it anywhere. Suits me fine. He'll be even more stressed when he finds out I'm here. And alive!*

"Hello, Jack."

Tommy looked up, not immediately associating 'Jack' with himself. He stared in total disbelief. Sharkey! But it couldn't be. Bruce took care of him.

"Thought I was rotting in the Mojave, did you?"

Tommy didn't say anything. He was trying to come to terms with the fact that the man standing in front of him was indeed Jim Sharkey. He had no way out. Except bluff. The kind that always stood him in good stead at the poker tables.

"Oh my god, Jimmy, I thought you were dead."

"Yeah, you failed Jack."

"No! I did not do it. You fell foul of a Vegas criminal gang. It had nothing to do with me."

"Don't fuck around with me, Jack."

Sharkey continued to call him Jack.

"I am not. I'm glad you're alive. I tried to find you. To get the money to you. But I learned you were dead. So I had no choice. I knew if H-R found out, they'd be after me. I had to run."

"And they are after you, Jack. They know I'm dead. Lucky me. So you've got them all to yourself."

"They were holding my dad hostage back there. There was a shoot-out. He's dead."

"And you ran. I thought if I found you that I would kill you. But you're not worth it, are you Jack?"

At this, Tommy got up from the table and handed his case to Jim.

"There's a million and a half in there. Take it."

Sharkey was taken aback. This ploy took the wind out of his sails. He looked over Tommy's shoulder and thought he was seeing things again. Another vision. Another mirage. He rubbed his eyes but it didn't go away. There she was. Emerging from the ladies room at the rear. The same ethereal vision. But she was real.

What the fuck, he thought, *a million will go a long way. Tommy is finished. H-R will get him in the end. He's only deluding himself. They'll get him.*

He kept the case, backed up towards the bar, and turned to walk away.

Three things happened then. The front door swung open and Hubert, holding the Walther in his hand, strode into the bar. At the same time, the ethereal girl had now reached Tommy and he cried out *"Gemma, Gemma!"* as she plunged a large kitchen knife into him, repeatedly. He fell, blood oozing from his lips, his throat gurgling the death rattle.

At that moment, a man with a camera stepped out of the shadows. The flashes lighted up the scene as he photographed the killing. A paparazzi. Then he disappeared.

Two customers grabbed Gemma and held her as the bartender dialed the cops. Hubert turned around and left immediately.

Jim Sharkey moved faster. Better to leave before the cops arrived. Back in his Escort, he opened the case and saw the batches of bills inside. He had no doubt there was over a million in sterling there. *A door prize*, he thought, *hell of a time for humor.*

Sixty-three

Hampstead Heath, London

Arfur's car was exactly where he said he'd be. Inside Hampstead Heath, only a stone's throw from Tom Gordon-Smith's home. *Arfur* had not heard any of the shooting even though Big Ned's men had not used silencers. He was lying back in his seat, head propped on a cushion, and shades over his eyes; the kind that airlines used to issue to passengers. His snooze was interrupted by a *tap, tap, tap* on his window. Waking, startled, he saw Hubert's face at the window and he relaxed. Checked his watch: two am. Thought: *not too late, could have been worse.*

He got out and held the door open for Hubert and Harvey. In the dim light he couldn't see the exhilaration on their faces and the look of manic joy in their eyes. He only heard their voices. As steady and calm as usual.

Two blankets and two glasses of hot whiskey awaited them in a thermos flask. Sipping the whiskey as *Arfur* pulled out of the Heath, they felt that Gemma had cheated them.

Sixty-four

Back in McDara's house, Sharkey pours himself a very large whiskey and sinks into one of the most comfortable chairs. The case sits on the coffee table, looking at him. He can feel his body change gear. He's been consumed by nothing but the need for revenge against Jack Miller. Always Jack Miller to him. And now it's over. He feels deflated. Cheated. He had wanted to torture Miller. Even kill him.

But he realizes that he couldn't do it. He stares at the case. He doesn't really want the money. But he can't give it back. Give it back to whom. H-R was built on the spoils of political criminals. Give it to charity. He thinks about that and decides that he, himself, is the most deserving charity. He laughs at that. But what do I do with a million sterling?

Owen will know. I must tell him what has happened. He picks up the phone and dials.

"Owen, it's over."

"God, you sure know how to say it. What is over?"

"Miller is dead."

"Did you kill him?"

"I wanted to. But I couldn't."

"Ok, what happened?"

So Jim starts at the beginning, finding Tommy's jag in the lock-up, learning about his indebtedness to the east London crime boss, Big Ned Simms, staking out Big Ned's house, seeing the arrival of Simm's thugs and the man himself, Tommy Gordon-Smith.

At this point, he takes a breather and sips his whiskey.

"Which one of my whiskeys are you drinking?"

"*Highland Park* this time. Think I need to replace your *Talisker*."

They both laugh at that. Refreshed, Jim continues his update, telling Owen how he had followed all of them from Big Ned's house to Tommy's father's house in Hampstead. Wondering what it was all about. Then the shootout, the guys fleeing the house, finally following Tommy to *The Duke of Hamilton* pub in the village.

"Who was the woman?"

"I don't know. He called her Gemma before she stabbed him."

"I guess he was the victim of revenge at the end."

"That's my guess. A jilted lover. A ghost from his past. But it'll all hit the news real soon."

"What do you mean?"

"Some paparazzi had followed her. And got lucky. Took pictures of her stabbing Tommy. Then he fled."

"You're not in these photos?"

"No, no. I was halfway to the door when it happened."

They ponder that as Jim finishes off his glass of Highland Park.

"Owen, what do I do with the money?"

"Put it in my safe. I will have my investment manager deal with it. He manages the international portfolio for GMA –

Global Management Investments – my old company. He'll invest it in your name. Equities, bonds, commodities, whatever."

"I sure owe you."

"No, you don't. Just get your ass back here."

The call ended, Jim decides not to refill his whiskey. Time to stay in command of himself. He goes on-line immediately and books a British Airways flight to Boston for departure the next day. *Nothing to keep me here*, he says to himself.

Sixty-five

Climbing out of London City Airport and finally airborne, Hubert and Harvey congratulate themselves.

"Another successful mission."

"Ah, but we had some help on this one."

"The jilted girlfriend."

By this time, the murders in Tom Gordon-Smith's house had made headlines in all the papers.

The Daily Scoop had 'scooped' all the tabloids. Gemma's murder of Tommy in *The Duke of Hamilton* boosted the second installment of the *Gemma Sinclair Story* to Page One. Sandy Thomas had become a star.

"Yes, but we'll still take the credit. Horst will find a way to claim the money that Tommy wired to the bank in Zurich. The rest is lost. But the money was never H-R's prime objective."

"No, they wanted blood."

"And we provided it."

Laughing together, they settled in at 35,000 feet for a smooth Atlantic crossing. They were expected at Teterboro Airport; their limousine driver would have them home a couple of hours after landing. Time for a night-cap and a catch up with the box set of their favorite program: *24 with Kiefer Sutherland: Live Another Day.* Set in London, they looked forward to this one. It seemed so fitting.

Three months later ...

H-R 'sorry' for aiding Paraguayan crime lords, rogue states and terrorists

Executive quits in front of US Senate as the Himmler-Ramos owned Miami Bank faces massive fines for laundering money for ODESSA cartels, pariah states, and criminal enterprises.

Executives with the Himmler-Ramos owned commercial bank in Dania, Florida, were subjected to a humiliating onslaught from US senators on Tuesday over revelations that staff at its Miami bank laundered billions of dollars for cartels, criminals and pariah states.

Lawmakers hammered the Paraguayan owned bank over the scandal, demanding to know how and why it had participated in financing a "pervasively polluted" culture that persisted for years.

A report compiled for the committee detailed how H-R subsidiaries transported billions of dollars of cash in armored vehicles, cleared suspicious travelers' checks worth billions, and allowed cartels to buy planes with money laundered through Cayman Islands accounts. Other subsidiaries moved money from Iran, Syria and other countries on US sanctions lists, and helped a Saudi bank linked to al-Qaida to shift money to the US.

Particularly scathing criticism was directed at large global banking giant, MetroBank, which acted as a correspondent bank for H-R and, in doing so, facilitated the movement of laundered funds. MetroBank lawyers protested vehemently.
Eduardo Himmler-Ramos, Chairman of H-Rs Miami Bank resigned before the committee.

About the Author

Pat Mullan was born in Ireland and has lived in England, Canada and the USA. He now lives in Ireland. He has published articles, poetry and short stories in magazines such as *Crannóg, Buffalo Spree, Tales of the Talisman, Writers Post Journal.* His short story, *Galway Girl,* was short-listed for the WOW Awards and was published in the new WOW Magazine in Galway in April 2010. Recent work has appeared in the anthologies, DUBLIN NOIR (published in the USA by *Akashic Books* and in Ireland and the UK by *Brandon Books), City-Pick DUBLIN* (published by *Oxygen Books* in 2010 to mark Dublin being chosen as UNESCO'S City of Culture for 2010), and *NOIR by NOIR West* (from Arlen House) in 2014.

His first novel, *The Circle of Sodom,* received two nominations, one for Best First Novel and one for Best Suspense Thriller, at the *Love Is Murder* conference in **Chicago.** His second novel, *Blood Red Square,* was published in the US and a new edition is now available on-line as a paperback and as an eBook. His latest novels, *Last Days of the Tiger* and *Creatures of Habit* are available on-line as eBooks on Amazon Kindle, Barnes & Noble's Nook, Kobo, and elsewhere; they are also available in paperback.

He is a member of *International Thriller Writers, Inc.*

Read all about him and find his novels, poetry, short work (and art) at: *www.patmullan.com*